THE CABIN

Jules Pardo

THE CABIN

Jules Pardo

DIAMOND HOUSE PUBLISHING

2014-08-27

Copyright © 2014 by Juliana Perez Sanchez

ISBN-13: 978-0-9938760-0-4

THE CABIN

First edition 2014-08-27

DIAMOND HOUSE PUBLISHING
diamondhousepublishing@hotmail.com

*For My Wonderful Mother and
Amazing Brother*

Chapter One

Sirens pierced through the morning silence, disrupting its tranquillity. The cold winter sun was slowly raising in the foggy sky, illuminating the morning calmly. However, it was brusquely replaced by robust red and blue lights, which torturously killed the soft glowing light of the sunrise. Alternating from red to blue, blue to red, they took over the streets, imposing themselves. Aggressively, the red lights tinted every street with the promise of tragedy as the serenity of the blue lights confirmed it all.

The once still morning air now had a soft winter breeze floating through the streets, serene and sweet. It traveled around the town as every street rapidly filled with police officers and firefighters. They began shouting at the top of their lungs before even stepping out of their vehicles. Some shouting commands through megaphones.

They went from house to house banging on doors and shouting.

"Everyone needs to evacuate the area immediately!"

"Everyone needs to leave now!"

"Evacuate the area immediately! I repeat, evacuate the area immediately!"

Confused people ran everywhere in their pajamas, winter coats and boots.

In the few minutes they had, they tried to grab everything they could, leaving a largely unbounded mess behind them. They were like tornados of despair.

Mothers held on tightly to their children. Some held on to their children's coats so tight, their knuckles turned white. Fear burned deep in their eyes as they gazed down at their children. From their mother's side, the children's faces varied from terrified to amusement.

For some, it was a game; a game the whole town was playing.

Some were scared and confused clinging hard to their mother's hand.

A very few seemed to grasp the gravity of the situation.

The once soft breeze gradually began growing stronger and stronger influencing the police officer and firefighters' shouts to become more and more violent, more and more demanding.

The now powerful wind found solace in the men's aggressive impatience.

By midmorning, the tranquillity and serenity had been completely replenished by sirens and screams, confusion and terror.

It all blended into a melody of chaos at its very finest. Over the chaotic noise, a police officer ferociously impatient roared,

"Everyone has to leave now!"

"A deadly storm is coming" another police officer chimed in with the same impatience.

"No one will survive this storm," a firefighter added.

"We are not prepared for it," another one said, his voice muffled a little by the chaotic melody.

"LEAVE NOW!" They all yelled violently in unison.

Terrified, the already hurried townsmen now accelerated their pace, going from running to sprinting in panic.

Adrenaline rushed through the streets, consuming the townsmen's spirits, consuming their every pulse beating through their hearts.

THE CABIN

Colored blurred movement occupied every inch of the streets, of the eye. It was all like an abstract painting.

Only every now and then would the eye catch a perfect clear picture.

A mother reassuring her child in her arms and kissing its head sweetly.

A husband reassuring his wife squeezing her hand and looking into her eyes.

Someone helping an elder or offering a ride to a complete stranger.

A man walking furiously, mumbling to himself the absurdities of life, of the situation, of everything.

A woman terrified clutching her rosary, praying as she looked around and move forward.

Lastly, in the middle of the progression of people marching, in the middle of chaos and misfortune, a perfect clear picture of two hands holding each other, promising

never to let go. In the middles of the confusion and blur, two hands proclaimed and
proved eternity.

≈

By ten in the morning, the town was now
deserted. Only two whole hours after the
evacuation had begun. It was bizarre, only
a couple of minutes before, the streets had
been an abstract painting accompanied by
the opera of chaos and confusion. Slowly,
the streets had begun to dim and then in
the blink of the eye it was empty, silent and
abandoned.

No one left.

No cars. No police officers or firefighters.
No families. No lovers. No individuals.

Nothing.

Looking towards the right, far ahead near
the horizon, were the last cars to have left
town, racing in the opposite direction of

THE CABIN

the coming storm. Far behind, some still at the edges of town, were all those who had no other choice than walk. They hurried as fast as they could.

The wind had grown colder and biting. It rattled aggressively the windows in unison with the walkers. It bit, pushed and slapped them, slowing their progression, but they still marched forward.

Self-preservation was stronger than the wind.

They marched forward fighting to live, to survive. The wind tormented their every step but they marched and marched until the wind was the only occupant of the town. It claimed the town, opening and closing doors with all its force. The wind became the dictator of the town. It brutally made sure no one or nothing could contest it.

Caught in the mist of the wind, posters were savagely ripped apart. Plastic bags fought and flew in protest against the wind. Everything, which was left lying around, flew against the wind in honor of the posters. Furious, the wind mercilessly defeated them. Then the wind proved its authority of dictatorship by making its conquest break and scratch windows, vandalizing the town against their will.

However, it was not enough. The wind had bigger plans. It wanted more territory. Gradually, it determinedly began to expand.

At its side, snow accompanied it, falling from every direction.

⚘

Miles away from the town, a cabin suddenly emerged from the thick blinding white falling snow. In the middle of the

THE CABIN

whiteness, it stood glorious and powerful despite the solitude, which haunted the grounds.

The cabin was quite large and made out of solid wood. It had couple of windows and seemed very stable. Small windows contoured the cabin. There were three windows on each side of the cabin and one in front and one at the back but they were situated fairly high.

Through the window on the sides, inside the cabin, it was large empty room except for numerous chairs and candles. The candles were all dispersed around the room. The chairs were all randomly placed, facing every direction. Some faced one another while other were back to back. Three chairs formed a circle to one side of the cabin, close by a window. Others formed small cluster of chairs and some were side by side. The rest of the chairs were scattered around the room, completing it, in a random perfection.

The double door entrance was unlocked.

It was better than having to stay outside in the blizzard.

As the storm got closer and closer, the wind grew more and more brutal. The wind lifted the snow of the ground and combined it with the already falling snow, blinding everything into a moving whiteness. White was everywhere.

Up. Down. Left. Right.

The wind pulled and tore people into the direction of the cabin.

People tumbled and crashed into the cabin. Touching the walls, they walked around to find the doors.

Each person who entered took a couple of seconds to regain their breath, some leaning against the close door once they were inside. They looked exhausted and

THE CABIN

beaten up but relieved neither the wind nor the snow could touch them anymore. Gradually, the cabin began to fill. At first, the people took seats far from one another but as the last few entered, they took their seats hesitantly next to strangers. As the last person walked in, a man with frozen eyelashes and covered head to toe with snow. The doors shut violently behind him.

Angry that it had lost his prey, the wind blew around the cabin, desperately trying to find a new victim. Empty-handed and frustrated, the wind blew and blew against the cabin. In response, the cabin groaned but stood its ground.

The snowstorm had now caught up to the cabin. The walls fought to remain straight against the protesting wind. The windows trembled and shuddered as the wind hit them, menacing to destroy them in a million pieces.

Through the trembling windows, the snow and wind danced together.

A deadly dance.

They danced to the earsplitting scream of the wind. They swirled and twirled together, caressing every inch of each other. Becoming one and separating, and once more becoming one.

Dangerously beautiful and elegantly, they waltz around the cabin.

Inside, they watched their lethal performance. They went pale with fear, their bodies tense and their breaths came out quick and uneven. Their eyes never left the windows.

They desperately hung onto life as they watch their dance murder their hopes.

Hours, minutes, seconds may have gone by. Who would know?

As the sky became darker, the snow settled softly on the ground, bowing delicately

THE CABIN

and gracefully after its performance, snowing everyone in the cabin.

The wind grew quieter and quieter until everything became still and dead quiet.

Chapter Two

The night was calm. Deadly calm. Too quiet. Too still.

Never had there been such a night. It was strangely breathtaking.

Without a doubt, the most beautiful night.

A night to remember.

Breathes came out slow, even and peaceful. Eyes gazed into nothingness. Minds far, far away, back in time, in the future but not the present.

It was a night to reflect.

The calmness of the night cleared their minds and helped them think, really think. It was as if it stripped bare their souls letting them for once truly see themselves. As if it

THE CABIN

had put their souls in a mirrored room, everywhere they looked they had no choice but be faced with the truth. All they could do was ponder on their life, their soul, their thoughts and their memories.

Some trembled slightly uncovering who they truly were. It is sometimes better to believe they are a completely different person than who they truly are. They can believe they are happy and all. They can believe they are complete and need nothing.

The fear of knowing their lives have been complete lies, hit them hard like a being punched in the face. They trembled awaiting more hits to come. Fear hit them in their gut. Years of living a lie. Years wasted. Now what? Who were they now? All the journeys they took to find themselves, and it all turned out to be a bunch of lies? At some point, did they decide to believe the lie they had found in themselves?

Regret and what might have been vibrated of them with every tremor.

Some trembled with the possibilities of what if.

Others sat motionless, nothing betraying them except for the pain burning in their eyes. Years of pain, of loss. Their eyes betrayed their melancholic soul. They seemed to be the ones who smiled and laughed the most. The ones full of life. The ones who were the life of a party.

Some sat with content air to them. Life had not been fair or unkind. It had given them grand joy, in which they found themselves utterly unable to complain.

Very few had smiles on their lips with eyes filled with love. They only saw the kindness of life.

THE CABIN

Others had a bitterness to them. Anger radiated of them like the sun radiates heat. Rage and bitterness clouded their eyes like mud dirtying water.

Happiness?! What Happiness?!

Love?! What Love?!

Achievements?! What Achievements?!

Grieve betrayal and failure is what life had given them.

The remaining thought of the future. Eyes filled with untouchable hope. Hope of a better life.

Hope of love. Hope of success. Hope of happiness. Hope, hope, hope, and more hope. Hope spread though their souls, in their blood, in their heart. Hope was in their every breathe.

A perfect night.

Time went by, and then slowly voices began to emerge from the silence.

Chapter Three

Candlelight illuminated the cabin, giving warmth and enough light so everyone could see one another. As the last candles were lit, it eased a bit of the tension the darkness of the night had brought. They had placed all the candles strategically around the room, making it hauntingly borderline romantically lit. They had been lucky; a few had lighters and matches with them. The silence was tolerable in the candlelight. It made everything less daunting.

The silence stretched out more or less comfortably around them.

THE CABIN

Interrupting the silence, a male's voice resonated through the cabin, snapping people out of their reveries.

"I am angry," he said "Always angry. I am angry with those who are happy. I am angry with those who are angry. I am angry with myself. I am angry with others. I am angry at the economy and politics. I am angry I have money and others don't. I am angry that I am never satisfied and when I am, I am angry because there is always something wrong, a little mistake, it is never perfect. I am angry at my life. I am angry for being angry.

I am angry.

I feel, as though there is nothing I could do or someone else could do to help me. I have to accept, I have condemned myself to a life of angriness," he said pointing at

JULES PARDO

his heart. As he dropped his hand, he lifted his stare from the floor and gazed straight ahead thoughtful. He laughed a short bitter laugh bringing him back to the cabin and continued talking.

"The funny part is I don't want to change. I'd rather be angry than anything else. I think it's because it is easier to be angry. It is always easier… I mean to find happiness in general requires so much work and energy.

And for what?

It can all be lost in a second and then you have to reinvest in time and energy to be happy once again. I work for money, nothing else. I can rely on money to buy me happiness or so to speak. It may not be true happiness but I will settle with grazing superficial happiness.

THE CABIN

I think it is easier too, to be angry than sad and depressed. When you are sad, you are vulnerable and people can take advantage, the same way they can take advantage when you are happy. Being angry gives you; a certain control. People don't dare to use you out of fear you might hurt them or whatever. And being angry…." He brought his eyebrows closer to each other, deep in thought.

"Maybe… deep down, I enjoy being angry." He concluded sitting motionless, leaning forward with his forearms resting on his lap and his hands in fits.

He seemed to be in his late-twenties and in the candlelight, his eyes were amber. He had light brown short hair and was medium built. And there was a certain violence to him, which could easily be confused for strength.

Deep in thought, he seemed content with the realization he had just made but quickly his gaze went from content to rage. Many saw his reaction. In response of seeing his reaction, some fidgeted closer to the edge of their chairs, wanting to help him.

But there is no helping those, who do not want to be helped.

Not too far from him, a woman sat with her arms tightly crossed against her chest. She had her right leg crossed over her left and was shaking her right foot from side to side in a quick swift movement.

A handful of seconds after the man had spoken, her voice occupied every inch of

THE CABIN

the room and air, leaving nothing except the sound and feel of her voice.

"Well I am frustrated. I work hard. Risk my life even, to help the poor, to help the less fortunate. And all I get in return is them, those whom I helped," she said, pointing angrily at herself. "Stab me in the back!" She said, releasing her arms from her chest and raising them in exasperation. Her foot had stopped shaking when she had begun speaking but now she uncrossed her legs, slightly stomping her right foot as it hit the ground.

"I don't understand it! Everything was going so smoothly. Everyone seemed happy. Really happy if you ask me. I had achieve it all.

In only a matter of weeks, they would all have a better life. All that was missing was

JULES PARDO

the official vote of the people. I knew everyone was happy.

I was confident.

I knew the moment they would have to vote, everyone would jump up at a chance to have a better life. Which meant voting for my proposition. But no one, literally no one voted for my solution.

I have never felt so betrayed.

They had shared their pain, their dreams and hopes with me. I knew this is what they wanted. I built everything around them. I consulted them. I made sure this is what they wanted. But, instead of voting for me, they left me utterly alone against arrogant politicians.

Why?! Why didn't they vote!? Why!? Why waste my time with their sorrows,

THE CABIN

making me feel sorry for them!? What was the point!? What?! Do they enjoy pity!?

I was so frustrated...

Helping people doesn't work. People will just stab you in the back once they're in better positions or insecure. People are born to be backstabbers. They will backstab you at any chance they get. They will even do it for the fun of it.

Trust me. I know.

Humans are ungrateful. Grateful people only exist in fairy tales, along with happiness and love. Don't waste your time helping people. They won't appreciate it. Hypocrite beings" she said.

Bitterness rolled of her tongue with every word, surprising more than one. She gave a startling contrast with her long wavy blond hair, pale skin with pink cheeks and a childlike air to her overall appearance, when her words were like darts of bitterness and eyes bursting with hatred.

"At least your heart was in the right place. I mean you must have changed someone's life for good or been an inspiration. Don't you think it is better to remember the good instead of everything they did wrong to you?" Said a small brown-haired woman who sat across from her, slightly to her right.

The blond looked incredulous.

"Pfff you are so innocent. When you climb out of your fairy tale bubble and realize what the world is really like, call me," she said making a telephone with her hand, close to her ear and giving the brunette a false smile. "I bet you will be more disappointment than me." She

THE CABIN

finished saying smug and shooting bullets of hatred at the other woman.

The small brunette regarded her calmly and responded with tranquillity.

"Maybe, maybe not. There is nothing wrong in only wanting to see the good part of life. I am not going to pretend as if I never suffered but why remember that pain over and over again. Why would I make myself relive that pain through the memory? Why should I obsess on the world's imperfection instead of its perfections? I enjoy life for what it is. I enjoy remembering the good time, the laughs" she smiled at a memory. A small laugh escaped from her lips.

"My favorite memory is when I had just graduated from university, and my friends and I decided to go on a road trip to this beach which was far, far, far away.

I think everything that could have gone wrong did. But oh did we laugh when we finally made it. I think we laughed for several minutes nonstop. Those who walked by us were probably thinking we were crazy but we didn't even notice them, we didn't care.

For that whole weekend, we were just the four of us on that beach with our happiness. Everyone else just vanished from our thoughts. It seemed like our whole trip was from a movie or book. We told and retold the whole journey, seeing it from different angles. Every time laughing so much our stomachs and cheeks hurt. We laughed at our reactions and ourselves. It was incredible. We met

THE CABIN

great people but most importantly, it was the trip I met my husband."

As she said it, she placed her hand on her husband's lap, her sweet smile turning sweeter as she gazed into her husband's eyes. He smiled back with so much affection that everyone could only stare in awe.

Staring back into her eyes, he said, "My favorite memory is when I saw this girl laughing away without a care in the world. I fell in love with her instantly.

Love at first sight.

Never before had I been so happy when I found out I was seating next to her on the bus back to the city four hours away. And with greatest luck, she fell in love with me on that bus ride." He leaned in, kissed her cheek, and stared at her lovingly.

JULES PARDO

"From that moment on, I promised her I would do anything to make her happy. I love her so much." His voice dropped to a whisper, a pained whisper and he turned his head to the side, unable to gaze at his wife and said "But I can't give her children.

I am so sorry sweetie.

I'm sorry."

He broke into loud sobs. The small brunette tried to calm him but he could not calm down. Everyone turned away, giving them some privacy. As much as the room allowed, although they still listened, everyone listened carefully.

"I am sorry. It's because of me we can't have children. I can't give you the only thing you've ever really wanted. It's my fault," he said, through sobs.

THE CABIN

"Shhh… Sweetie, you are everything I want. I want a happy life with you. I don't want you to regret anything or feel bad," she said sweetly.

"And it's not your fault. Have a little faith. Everything will be okay"

"But I failed as a husband…"

"No. Honey you haven't failed in anything."

"Yes I have I …"

"No."

"Yes. I…"

"No. You nothing ok—"

"Exactly!" He exclaimed interrupting her, "That's what I am. Nothing. I am…"

"NO! GOSH!" She yelled interrupting him now. "I had planned out a perfect way to tell you this but since of the storm I couldn't do it tonight the way I wanted, so

JULES PARDO

I thought I'd wait. But here it goes anyways," she said in frustration. "You are not a failure. Okay? You are everything! And you will be a dad!" She half yelled.

"I am pregnant," She said, her voice becoming sweet, warm and motherly. It rang with uncontainable happiness. Tears of joy ran down her cheeks.

He stared into her glowing eyes, searching and took her face into his hands, wiping away a tear from her cheek with his thumb.

"We are pregnant?"

She caressed his brown hair and whispered lovingly "Yes, we are pregnant"

He bent down and kissed her smiling lips with all the tenderness of the world. Staring into her eyes, he put her at arm lengths studying her again and abruptly

THE CABIN

lunged to give her a hug, his tears turning into tears of joy. He laughed softly and whispered in her ear. An even bigger smile spread through her face.

Everyone else turned to look at them happily. Some got up to congratulate them, other simply smiled at them adoringly from their seats.

Everyone was happy to hear the news of a newborn.

The idea of a newborn. A new life, a new chance. No matter how much some could hate life or be cynical, a newborn is joyful news because a newborn is survival. It is an instinct far too grand to be ignored or simply disliked or dismissed. A newborn is a new chance at humanity. Maybe if they all did it right, humanity would survive and live their dreams. Maybe everything would

JULES PARDO

be better. Each generation is a generation of hope. A hope, which seems to die when they begin to compare themselves, to want more than they should, to let greed govern them and to forget others feel and are humans just like them. A hope, which dies when all respect, is lost for others and for nature.

But, everyone still hopes.

A newborn is more than the future, it is more than just hope that everything could be better; a newborn is the proof of "Once upon a time, they were two people who loved each other undeniably and created a new life together and the newborn went on to…." Whatever comes after that, it doesn't matter. What matter is, each newborn is the only proof humanity has

THE CABIN

loved, desired and lived a turmoil of emotions.

Everyone was silent, deep in thought once more. However, this time around, their souls had a content air.

Everyone except one.

He fidgeted in his seat, his expression switching from sadness to anger to hope and once again sadness, anger and hope.

"Why am I so angry?" He began after a while.

"I don't understand it. I hear and see all those who are angry and bitter and I don't want to end up like them. I want to be happy.

I try to change; I try to remain calm, not let anger get the better of me. But I can't sometimes… And I end up hurting those

JULES PARDO

around me and then I get even madder but at myself.

I don't want anger to control my life. I try to control my anger. I really do. Whenever I start feeling angry, I take deep breaths, I try to think happy, calming thoughts. But on some occasions, out of nowhere, midway through inhaling, I explode. I lose all self-control. I lose... I lose myself to anger.

Don't get me wrong. I am happy and grateful for my life but I want to be happy like them" he pointed at the small brunette and husband, who had joy written or rather stamped all over them.

"They have problems. We all do. They know life can be cruel and they are still happy and only remembering the good. And it seems because they do, good things

THE CABIN

happen to them. At the end of my days, I only seem to be able to remember the bad stuff, the things I did wrong, which happens to be everything. I find it so hard to remember the good, especially the good side of people, all I can ever recall is all the bad or negative things about them.

I wonder if I have a unconscious reason to be mad. If so, it had better be a good one because I don't want this for me. I don't want anger to rule me or influence me. I don't want my temper to get in the way of my relationships. I want a happy life filled with love and bliss...

I dream that one day I will meet a woman and we will fall deeply in love. I dream she will save me from myself. She will cure my angriness. She will make me a better

JULES PARDO

person. I dream we will live happily ever after.

I hope it's not too much to ask for.

I... I just hope she will see past my outbursts and see the man I am" He finished saying.

He seemed hopeful, but deep in his dark eyes, there was doubt. As the seconds pass by, the doubt in his eyes become, more and more pronounced.

It became a battle between hope and doubt.

It seemed like he wanted to believe everything would work out but the cynical part of him simply would not let him. He let out a sigh of exasperation, dropping his head in defeat.

THE CABIN

Sensing someone was staring at him, the man looked up to see his neighbor looking at him.

His seating neighbor was a young man, who seemed to be the same age as him, mid-twenties to late twenties. He stared at the other man turning his body to face him. His gaze was intense but not in an uncomfortable way. The young man's eyes held too much passion and excitement for it to be uncomfortable. It was almost like staring into a child's eyes. When he spoke, words tumbled out of his mouth hurriedly, as if he was scared he would not be able to express everything.

He put his hand on the other man's back reassuringly and said, "Never give up man. No matter what happens. Never give up. I am telling you she is out there, closer than you think."

Dropping his hand form the other man's back, he turned his body in his chair to face forward and then he said in his peculiar way of speaking "I almost gave up on the whole idea of love, of having that special someone who you can trust and spend the rest of your life taking care of each other. I am glad I didn't. I found the woman who is perfect for me. The moment we met, we clicked.

Although it took us, a couple of years for us to realize what we felt for each other was more than friendship. She is everything I ever needed and wanted. She loves me for me. She knows every demon I possess and she still loves me unconditionally. She knows me better than

THE CABIN

she knows anyone else and I know her better than I know myself.

I couldn't be happier." He smiled hugely.

"We are getting married in a couple of months. I can't wait to officially begin my life with her as husband and wife. And we are excited about starting a family together.

I am ready to be a father. I am sure there will be hardships down the road but I just hope my child will think I am the best dad ever. I know she will be the best mom ever to our children.

One of the best thing is we have always wanted a family. Can you imagine starting a family with the person, you love most and who is your best friend?

I still can't get my head wrapped around it.

JULES PARDO

I will be a husband soon and hopefully" he crossed his index and middle finger, "a father, shortly after our wedding.

I am so glad she missed this snowstorm, and is safe. I love her so much. She is more than I ever dreamed for," he said lastly.

Words tumbled out of his mouth, not out of fear, he would not be able to express everything he wanted but rather because it was in his nature to be passionate, to stare with passion, to speak with passion. The excitement and eagerness of his voice caused his words to rush out in the cabin's air; it caused his body to become firm and expressive as he rambled on. As he finished speaking, he relaxed into his chair, smiling widely and turning his head to gaze at the other man, giving him this time, a reassuring smile.

THE CABIN

In the same second, the silence was interrupted by a loud grunt. Instinctively, everyone turned towards the noise. It was a small boy, the only child in the cabin in fact, who had grunted in utter disgust. He was around twelve years old. He had black penetrating eyes, in which many emotions raced one after the other, like a never-ending race. Although he managed to keep his stare solid.

"Ugh" he grunted again with his upper lip curled up in disgust.

"It's pathetic. All you adults make me sick. You all want to have a family, you all want kids, love and blah, blah, blah. Love doesn't last and you don't even understand the responsibility of having a kid.

JULES PARDO

At first parents are good parents. They are attentive to what the baby needs and they still love their husband or wife. It is all new and so exciting and everything.

But after the kid hits a certain age, all of a sudden parents become selfish. They forget they even have a kid to take care of. It all becomes about them. Their happiness and what they want. To top everything off, they want the kid to understand everything because it is a "part of life".

What about, what I want? What about, what children want?

That's not important.

To my parents, it was never important. All they cared about was themselves and how they felt. "I am not happy," he said mimicking a high pitch female voice. "They always fought because they weren't

THE CABIN

happy. I wasn't happy either but that wasn't important.

I was invisible to them," he paused indifferent, with pain deep in his soul.

"They never tried to fix their relationship. They let it just died. When things got worse, I was the reminder of their unhappiness. Near the very end though, I suddenly became desirable. They began fighting over who loved me more.

They say they love me but I don't believe them." He inhaled miserable.

"Four years ago they got divorced. Just two weeks before I turned eight. No one told me it was really happening. I heard a few words here and there but I..." He laughed in disgust.

It's sickening. I still hoped they would work it all out. I hoped they would

JULES PARDO

remember why they were together in the first place or at the very least for my sake they wouldn't divorce. They wouldn't break our family apart.

It wasn't always all bad, we were just a normal family before or I like to think but I can't remember.

I found out the day my father left. He sat across from my mother and me. My mother sat next to me her arms wrapped around me, giving me gentle strokes on my arms and back during the whole conversation. She never looked at me, not even once while he talked. She just glared at my father as he explained why he and my mother were getting a divorce. And even though I told him I knew what getting divorced meant, he still explained everything in detail.

THE CABIN

Too many details…

I knew what it meant," he said angrily "One of my friends parents got divorced the year before. It had been a complete surprise to him because they had always been a happy family. He had memories of them being happy together, of his parents looking at each other with love and stuff.

I wasn't surprised. I was just hurt that I wasn't enough for them to be together or important to them." His face held all the hurt and anger of several lifetimes. It was painful from them to witness his hurt. So young and he already experienced so much pain. He would have to carry it with him whether he wants it or not, for the rest of his life. He has no choice. No one gave him a choice.

JULES PARDO

"My grandmother moved in with my mother and me after the divorce. You know, to help take care of things and me but after a while, it was just my grandmother, who took care of me. She did the best that she could but it wasn't her job to do it. She is very old. It's unfair for her and me. I don't know, I thought since I couldn't have a real family, at least I deserve a real mother who takes care of me. After all, she fought so hard to prove she loved me more to keep me. But she is too busy finding me a "new daddy." She says I need a good male role model, implying my father isn't. I know it's not for me she does it. I think she is afraid of being old and alone. She goes out on most weeknights and every weekend religiously.

THE CABIN

Sometimes she manages to bring home a "new daddy."

They never last.

Thanks to custody, every Saturday I have to spend time with my father and his new wife.

It is degrading.

They spend time with me without paying attention to me. Nothing I do ever gets their attention. All they want to do is play happy family just like my mom and her boyfriends. I don't want to play happy family. I want one.

I hate them. They ruined my life. All I want is a family, a normal family living under the same roof. A family like the ones you see on TV or at least one of those families where the parents are divorced, but they are still friends and talk to each other and the kids are happy and everything.

Aren't adults supposed to be wise and responsible? Why aren't you responsible?" He asked bitterly, staring pointedly at everyone.

"Parents are wise, parents know best" he said in a mocking voice and then grunted once more in disgust.

"Blah, blah, blah! I hate them. They ruined everything. They ruined my life. It sucks to live in this world. I hate my life. I wish I were never born, that it would end now. I hoped the storm would have granted my wish. I hate life, I just hate it with all my guts," he said almost on the verge of crying. He looked around mad and hateful.

THE CABIN

"I hate life," he said again but this time daring someone to say something back. Although, his tone ended any argument or comment that might have been said on his behave. The boy was pleased no one spoke, no one fought back but deep in his black eyes, a child screamed for attention, for a reaction, for anything.

He got nothing.

As the silence continued he became more pleased, more hurt.

A man across the room, who appeared to be in his fifties, stared at the boy. At first with disbelieve, but it slowly changed into compassion. Studying the boy, the man spoke the words of his soul.

"Life is not how I would have ever imagined nor thought it would be like. After a while, you think you know what will

JULES PARDO

happen next and yet life always seems to find a way to surprise us. It surprises us in ways we never thought possible. Is it a good or bad thing? I wonder.

I believe life is the decisions we make. Every decision has its consequence. I think every consequence is good, no matter how big or bad it may seem at first. When something bad happens, you learn something new and become wiser. You can better understand the concept of life and you are able to comprehend human nature and appreciate nature.

Life is made to make mistakes. Life is wonderful. It is painful. It is joy, it is fear and it is a mystery. Life goes by in the blink of an eye; it goes so fast yet unbearable slow. Life is love, nature. It is infinity. Life is in a small child's laugh, in the breeze going

THE CABIN

through the trees in summer, in the sound of music. Life is everything that happens around us, it is breathing, it is existing and it is emotional. Life is a smile. It is a kiss of passion, a stare of affection, a caress of love. Life is about discovering everything and nothing.

Life is the dance between cultures and beliefs. It is the solo of independence and the choreography of dependence. Life is the dance of the beliefs the heart holds dearly and the facts the mind stands by determinedly. It is the dance of joy and sorrow, of people, of relationships and hardships...

Life is what you make it. No one can do it for you or tell you have to live it a certain way because at the end of the day, life is you.

JULES PARDO

Take your passion and make something out of it. Go out and meet new people, try to be unforgettable in the best way possible. Try to find that special someone who will make your heart swell with love. And when you finally find the perfect one for you, give them all your love without hesitation or regret. Make life worth it, so every morning you wake up with a smile on your face, happy a new day has come. Make life an adventure worth living.

Life is worth living.

For me, life is trying new things and savoring each breath. I have learned to love the element of surprise, of not knowing what will happen, of not knowing anything except whatever it might be happiness or pain, life is worth the uncertainty.

THE CABIN

The future is worth it.

Of course, I suffer but I learn from it. I learn who I am and my emotional limits as well as my physical limits. I enjoy life and everything it has to offer. As tempting as it is to throw everything away for the sake of getting rid of the pain, don't because life always has something better to offer you down the road. Life is on your side. It is always loyal to you. Believe in it and be patient. Life is a gift. Life is you. Life is filled with choices only you can make." As he spoke, he stared into the boys eyes.

They stared at each other for a couple of seconds, their eyes never moving, not even a millimeter, a force passing through them.

Wordless communication.

JULES PARDO

Then it was over. He stared into the boy's now wide-open eyes. The boy was shaking lightly, fight back tears. In his eyes, his never-ending race of emotions vanished as recognition won the gold metal. The man gave him a warm smile, a smile that hugged the boy affectionately. He nodded and gave the man a shy smile back.

The man could not make up for the parents behavior nor could he judge but he gave the inner screaming child of the boy, something no one had dared to give him, when he desperately needed it most.

Importance. Time. Compassion.

A reaction.

Chapter Four

He sat in the corner of the cabin. The candlelight barely touching his features. In the darkness, profound still eyes surveyed the gathering. Once... twice... a third time. He inhaled sharply and his baritone voice carried throughout the cabin.

"We are animals, controlled animals. We are controlled by our minds and therefore we are perfect. But in a moment of pure rage, of pure despair, we become true animals, letting our instincts take over.

Everyone is quick to judge when we lose that control. They judge with every fiber of their beings and don't realize it happens to them too. We cannot see our errors but we see all those in others perfectly. We never make any mistakes; it is always others who do. When a crime has been done, all those not included judge heartlessly. They believe they have right because they know best, because they know everything. They only see a victim and a predator. They only need and want a victim and predator. It is always a victim and a predator. Never two victims or two predators. There is always a need to have a bad person in every scenario.

To them, I was the predator, the villain, the bad person. To them, I knew what I was doing but I... I barely remember what happen. You don't think when your instincts take over, you just find yourself doing certain movements, certain words come out of your mouth and everything is a blur. Your vision, your surroundings, it all become

THE CABIN

blurry. All the noise around you is replaced by the pounding of your heart in your ears.

It is hard to remember.

One night of pure rage is all it took. I was intoxicated with rage. I felt all my blood and rage rush to my hands, then next thing I knew, I was a criminal. I wasn't drunk nor under the influence of drugs. Therefore, they condemned and judged me as a criminal who knew what he was doing, who did it on purpose, who according to lawyers had planned it. In a second, they condemned me forever as a criminal, unhuman. In that second, I lost all my rights as a human being to society.

I pay the price every day and will continue paying it. Not even death can liberate me. I am forever a criminal, forever the subject of heartless judgment. I won't be remembered by anything else. I am the criminal. I am not a murderer, far from it. I have never killed an animal or a person or anything but everyone judges me like I did.

You all judge me so hard but you don't understand, you don't know or care to know. Once you get an opinion in your head, once you've picked a side, everything said on behalf of the other falls on deaf ears.

You are hypocrites.

We live in a society where violence is part of the everyday life, yet it is a taboo. It is something not tolerated but done every day. Everyone loses their temper or have moments of violence, whether it's physical or verbal. But no one says anything to you.

You know... You are all more violent than I am. I made a mistake and I take full responsibility," he said pressing his palm to his chest, his hand strong and stiff. "I won't blame it on my past or seeing my father resolve everything with violence. I won't even blame it on the moment. I am not violent...

THE CABIN

I was just pushed to my extreme. It all built up in me and exploded.

But you... You are all so violent with your judgment. You don't even need a reason to be violent, you just are. Your words are like a thousand needles to the heart. With your words, you create beasts. Your words transform criminals into beasts. Then you think of them as animals, worthless.

Worthless animals.

And they deserve to suffer. We are humans. We have feelings. Can you understand that? The label "Criminal" doesn't change the fact that blood still pumps through our veins. Criminals are just like you. They were once you, just a simple, normal human being before your words transformed them into beasts, into criminals.

Does that mean they shouldn't be punished? No, I don't think so. I believe every "criminal" is responsible for their crime and should pay the price. No matter how big or small the crime was. But all the judgment which falls on behalf of criminals should be abolished or they should condemn all those who judge heartlessly as criminals as well..." he paused thoughtful.

He surveyed the cabin, looking at each individual. He pondered his thoughts. Seconds passed by. He sighed and said "But just be careful with your words and actions towards us and among yourselves.

I have seen a simple stare, a few simple words create an indestructible beast, an animal... a new criminal." His voice trailed off into the silence.

He barely spoke without resentment, without anger. Only on one occasion did his voice express a hint of anger. However, there was more hurt and powerlessness than actual anger in his speech. He simply spoke words filled with their own meaning, their own emotions, and their interpretation.

Everyone turned in their seats thoughtful, relaxing their backs on the back of their chairs, thinking. Their bodies tensed as they lost themselves deeper in thoughts. Thoughts, many thoughts. The man had given much to ponder on. They could not escape from contemplating.

Everyone judges, that's the tragedy of it. And like most things in life, it holds a negative and positive side.

Judgment comes too easy. It is sometimes disguised as helpful critiques but nevertheless, it is still judgment. It affects everyone. Grand ideas are never materialized out of fear, they will be judged.

Does judgment come from people believing they are superior and wiser, and therefore they have the right to "educate" others? Or does it come from people who are insecure and need protection, which they find in the judgment they give out?

There is too much judgment.

There is so much, it has become a normality. Judgment is degrading. Degrading another human is normal nowadays. No matter how big or small the judgment may be or how insignificant, it is still degrading another. It is discrimination. It is trying to prove the inferiority of another person.

But it is also, a good indicator on the morals and ethics a society holds. Judgments are the point of views a nation believes in. It is the indication of the nation's tolerance.

Not many nations are tolerant.

While they thought, in the center left of the cabin, a man sat deeply in thought, so deep his eyebrows smashed into each other. They hovered above his eyes creating shadows on his gaze. His eyes were a vivid green brightly shinning with emotions. He was not young nor old. Neither was he in between. Strange. However, his voice vibrated with life and experience as he spoke.

Silence extended out around the cabin until his voice vibrated through the air.

"Every day, I realize how much more injustices there are in this world. It never ends. Injustice here. Injustice there. So many. Too many. When I was little, I was well aware there were injustices but never would I have thought how many there are and how horrible they are.

There are so many injustices. It's endless. So much injustice, it is not fair. And to make everything worse, most of the time there is always someone taking advantage of every injustice, of the powerless situation the victims are in. They take advantage for their own profit or personal gain...

Whenever someone wants to help. I mean really help, not like those organizations that say "give us a donation today, so we can help these children or help get medical care for this diseases or something." I mean come on, don't you think by now, with all the money they received over the years, they would have solved, if not every problem at least most. There shouldn't be anyone in need any more. Period.

The thing is there is always someone who will take that money for his or her own benefit, whether it is the organization or the government. No one can change that fact. The money goes to them.

Of course, they give some money to the cause and it does some good but it's not enough. I guess they have to give a small percentage in order to be able to receive more money. But I firmly believe they keep most of the money for them.

Have you ever noticed how some "humanitarians" dress in designer clothes and want to discuss world hunger and poverty in a hundred and twenty dollar plate restaurant? But you can't hold that against them," he said. He pressed his lips tightly into a straight line, turning his head to the side and gazing at the cabin wall.

He shook his head and said, "You know what I don't understand whenever someone wants to help, get his hands dirty, spend one on one time with those in need. Those who are ready to take a bullet to save lives, to defend those in need, they somehow always end up getting killed or end up dying suddenly. There is always some accident or out of nowhere they get sick and the next day, they unexpectedly die. It always seems so fishy.

I guess someone feels threaten by them and they have the "power,"" he said, making quotation marks with his fingers in the air. "To order someone to kill whoever they wish, which is the true humanitarian who stands hand in hand with the people. I think they feel exposed by them and therefore it is intolerable and they must be eliminated.

Exposing someone as a fraud, as the bad person, exposing him or her for whom they really are —greedy people— is suicidal. Or simply just thinking differently, having your own opinion or having an opinion which opposes theirs and having the guts to speak them proudly is also suicidal."

He became thoughtful as the moonlight shone on him.

"It all just gets my blood really going," he said after a couple of seconds. "I get so mad. I wish I could help. I wish I could do something. But what can I do when organizations barely show results and yet they still are praised for their wonderful work? And if you go against those in power who do wrong, you know you will end up dying.

THE CABIN

They don't think about you or the fact you are a human trying to defend other humans or that you are a human just like them.

We are all the same. The only difference is, they only want money and you want to help those who guarantee they get money at the end of the day.

It infuriates me so much. I feel so hopeless. I get so angry that I go to manifestations. I get involved in acts of violence and everything, convinced it will bring peace. In the moment, I determinedly and strongly believe it's the solution, the only solution. But at the end of the day, I know it does no good in the long-term. It just condemns us to more fury, to more rage and ultimately to more violence. I hate violence. I hate harming anyone on purpose or not.

But those who take advantage... those who cause so much harm... I can't help but wish them misfortunes and a little bit of harm," he finished saying.

His green vivid eyes were contemplating his thoughts. His face pained. A few strands of dirty blond hair fell on his eyes as he settled deeper into his chair.

Candles burned and illuminated the cabin as if it too wanted to communicate, to tell a story or share its thoughts.

Through the windows, the moonlight infiltrated the cabin like a spotlight, curiously focusing powerfully on whoever was speaking. Moving around the cabin in a circle, it slowly shifted to the woman sitting behind the man who had spoken. As he talked, she had only been able to see the back of his head and every now and then catch a glimpse of his face when he turned his head to the right.

Now sitting completely back to back with him, looking outside the window, she said,

THE CABIN

"I know what they do is wrong and I am not trying to defend them. Please don't get mad at me or anything. But... I just wish, in general, people would see both sides to every story. I think if we did, we would understand, tolerate and respect everyone more. It would create more peaceful environment.

We expect them to see us as human beings but we don't see them as human beings. Why should they treat us with respect, if we don't treat them with respect?

They are humans like us. And just because they do more wrong than good doesn't make them less human. They are not that different from us. We all make different types of mistakes, that's all. I—"

"Oh great, you're on their side. You must be heartless. A heartless human being. Keep defending them. Keep going that lane and I promise you, you won't be here for long," the bitter childlike blond from earlier cut her off, staring at her with her blue eyes overflowing with so much hatred.

Taken aback, she took a couple of seconds to regain her control. When she did, she stared back determinedly at the other woman.

It was odd to see their stare exchange. They looked quite similar, both blond and blue-eyed with a delicate body. They had the same childlike air but like children, one was more outgoing and malicious, as for the other one, she was more reserved and calm.

The more reserved one said in a calm voice with a slight hint of annoyance. "I am not defending them, as I mentioned before, what they do is wrong but we need to see the human in them.

I know firsthand what it is like. My father was a politician. Most often than not we get

THE CABIN

mad at politician and classify them in the same category as all those who do wrong. We get mad at them because they promise and promise and promise they will do good things for the people, help whoever needs help but once they are in power they change.

They change because they have power.

All of a sudden, you get all this power you only ever dreamed about and it blinds you in its shinning bright glory. It's an under-whelming feeling. They try to help, really, they do but they can't make any decision alone. There are always people around them advising them to do other things. They will say it will be beneficial in some-way or another, if they do something else. Or simply not do what they promised be-cause it would hurt the people or some-thing like that, if they did. They convince them that somehow it will be better for the people.

I know you must think, "Why do they listen to them? They must know it is wrong, no?" Or "They should stand up to them and do what they promised."

But ask yourself this, if you had power, real power, would you risk losing it all? Imagine you can have a better life, you can offer your family everything they want. You know your children could have the best education, the best life you could ever offer them.

Would you really risk losing it all?

Honestly?

If you had the power, would you do what you promised and risk it all or would you be blinded by it?

Most get blinded and confused. The power consumes you in the blink of the eye. The last thing you see is the shining glory of it then everything is black. Blinded and confused, you have to trust the people you work with to guide you in the right direction, you have to work as a team. But not every team member has the best intentions.

Most start out with the best intentions. They really do, I know they do. Everyone does— well, let's be generous, more like ninety-eight percent of them, start out with the best intentions. They want to do what is right….

The thing is what you think is the right thing, may not be what others think is the right thing. Someone who was born in a nonviolent environment will think violence leads nowhere. But someone who was born into violence will firmly and proudly believe violence is always the solution, no matter the problem. Are they wrong? Can we blame either one of them? Disrespect them? The same happens in many different scenarios like politics, injustices and crimes. They try to help in most cases but there is always that conflict of what is right and wrong and who thinks which is which.

To top everything off is the money.

Would you turn down money?

Ideally and in theory, yes. However, in practice I don't think anyone or many of us at least would. We all need it because we have needs which demand financial support. We need money to survive, both physically and socially. We have debts to pay and whatnot. We have vices, which need monetary feeding. If you were handed a couple of thousand dollars, would you turn it down? If you knew where it came from, would it matter?

But what if you don't know where the money came from? I know it sounds impossible but I think that sometimes some people in those types of circles don't know where the money comes from. Many transactions are made behind their back. They believe they are doing everything they can with the budget they have. You know, some actually believe they are making a different. It may be true, they might be making a difference, but it's not enough for the world.

There are good people in those circles, who try to do good but we judge them all because a few handful actually want to do wrong and gain profit from it. And maybe because we judge them, they think, "Well if they think I steal or use the money for my own benefit, then fine, that's what I'll do." Then they do because they are hurt, because they feel judged.

Although you know, there is always that one person who wants money more than anything else in the world, who will do any-thing to get it. Can you blame him? I mean have you ever dreamed of having a big house, the newest car and clothes? Have you ever dreamed of having the luxury to travel whenever you want for mini-vaca-tions to luxurious places?"

At the end of the day, no one should die of hunger, war or injustices. No one should live miserably because of a government or whatever. But hating them, fighting against them won't do anything good, like he men-tioned before," she said, turning to point at the man behind her.

Their eyes met and something connected between them. Two souls finding each other becoming one soul of love. They smiled knowingly. They didn't need words. They didn't need confirmation. They knew. Their eyes filled with newfound love for each other. He silently urged her to continue.

Thoughtfully she said, "I think we need to understand one another and find a solution which benefits us all by talking not by violence or hate. We need to understand each side. We need to be open-minded and ask ourselves "What would I be like in their position and honestly answer the question. Many of us will see we are not that different from them.

We have to find a solution to all injustices. I believe we can by sitting down and talking" She finished saying and then added "One can hope and dream, right?"

She looked up and stared back at his vivid green eyes happily, he smiled back lovingly.

Seating with their arms pressing against the back of the chair side by side, they tenderly interlaced their hands together, lock-

ing their souls with love. They sat closely together, their thighs touching. And when he
thought no one was looking, he kissed the
top of her head softly and sweetly, then
whispering quietly in her ear.

Across the room, an elegant elderly
woman lunched without a warning into her
legacy.

"To want is a strange emotion. It is as
powerful as it is weak. To want is normal.
Sometimes we want small things, which we
forget with time or even in seconds. But on
some rare occasion, what we want blinds us
unto thinking it is a need. It becomes such a
powerful need, almost like air to our lungs.
The mere thought of it sends your heart
into a rapid palpitation. You feel your heart
squeeze and your breath comes out slightly
uneven...

This only happened to me once, and it got
me where I am now. To this day, I do not

know if it was the best or worst thing to have happened to me.

It all started right after I graduated from university. A week later, I got married with my boyfriend who I had been with for five years. When we got back from our honeymoon, I already had a job awaiting me. I was beyond happy. I had everything I ever needed. A loving husband and a good job. I simply could not complain.

I was ecstatic but that quickly disappeared.

I suddenly became restless.

I didn't know what was happening to me. I wasn't happy. I knew I should be happy but I just was not. I felt horrible. I was lying all the time to everyone, selling the idea I was happy. I felt like a lousy liar. They would give me looks as if saying we know you are lying, especially my husband. What was I supposed to say? Not even you are making me happy?

One day I passed in front of the CEO's office of my company and I was overcome with the desire to be CEO. I wanted to be in that chair, behind that big desk. I dismissed the feeling thinking, "of course everyone dreams of being the boss, the big boss. It is normal. Although, as the days went by, the sensation became more and more powerful. Every time I closed my eyes, I only saw myself behind that desk and all it came with. I envisioned everything. Especially the power.

I began working twice as hard and rapidly began moving up the ranks.

I also began wanting other things, such as designer clothes, shoes, and perfume. And of course, handbags. I only wanted designer items. Now that I was in higher level, I had

THE CABIN

to look the part. I was invited to dinner parties, to charity events and galas.

I had a car but I need the newest and most desired car in the market. I also needed a new house so I could host superb dinner parties. I could not be a gracious host in a small studio apartment.

Ever since I was little girl, I had a very determined mind. What I wanted, I got. Thus, I only taught myself to only want things I needed" She paused, a small smile forming on her lips. "I thought it would be less complicated like that.

I still remember like it was this morning when I realized I had everything I wanted. Everything I needed. I was the youngest CEO my company ever had. Not only did I have power over my company but we were also expanding which meant I had power over three different companies. The power of it all was intoxicating. I had a huge walk in closet filled with high-end designer names. My house... it was a mansion with a great big backyard, where I hosted the most grandiose parties. And I had the most desired car. I was living the dream everyone dreamed.

I inhaled glory and exhaled power.

I remember that day, I was walking through the park and for the first time in years, I was enjoying the sun on my skin. I was enjoying the sound of the children's laughter and the birds chirping away. In that moment, I realized I was happy, I was really happy.

I was happy once again.

It was something, which came from within. I knew I was happy because I had it all. Before, I would have not noticed the most beautiful or sunniest day.

I was consumed by desire, by my need of wanting it all. To me, every day was the same, the sky always a dull lifeless gray. All I could see was the sparkling image of me being CEO dressed in the latest designer gown, laughing away with a glass of champagne in my hand, at an important work event with my co-workers.

Years went by and everything stayed the same. I was invincible. I thought myself as an empire. An indestructible empire. But every empire have their downfalls.

My marriage became more a marriage of convenience rather than love or lust. I learned to turn a blind eye on his little nights out and long weekends. I can't bring myself to blame him or even be mad at him. I was not around. I did not pay attention to him. I did not give him what he needed and wanted. Therefore, he went elsewhere to obtain it. Lies became like breathing to us. Telling and accepting them was part of the everyday routine.

JULES PARDO

As the years went by, I kept wanting more and more but with every new desire came an aching emptiness from within. After I achieved my new desire, it took a week or sometimes less before it would lose its interest, leaving me wanting something else. I was never fulfilled. It frustrated me, although I would not have admitted back then.

I wanted completely different things for myself when I was a little girl but with the years, I kept lying to myself that this is what I have always wanted, no not wanted but needed.

My life continued in the same pattern, my downfalls growing deeper and deeper within me." She paused thoughtful.

"As I remember my life, I sometimes wish I could have had a tragic downfall. One where I lose everything and I realize it wasn't what I needed or wanted for myself.

THE CABIN

Or where I realize family is more important than material things. Therefore, I could pick myself up and move on.

I wish I had learned something from it all, so I would be wiser. So I could teach someone something like "the only thing in life which truly matters is love and relationships" or "the more you want the more you will be dissatisfied, it will never be enough." But I can't because I know I would not have trade it for anything in the world. Still would not.

You see my point? Even now, I would not change it. After everything, I have been through. Through all the pain I lived, I would actually recommend to go after your wants and needs, even if its material things or power. I would simply say it would be better than you ever imagined but also worse than you would have thought.

Does that make me inhuman? Heartless? Or something along those words?

The joy I felt when I realized I had it was so grand. So glorious, I wish everyone could experience it. I want to be able to say, I only want the basic out of life but I know they would fall on deaf ears. Everyone always wants the dream, wants more, a better life.

Is it wrong to want the dream? Is it wrong to want to be happy? Is it actually worth it? Question I have asked myself my entire adulthood. Was that joy worth this bitter-sweet taste I have while I await death to liberate me? I hope it was..." she looked around the cabin, registering everyone's expression.

"I know my story may seem odd and confusing. It has no moral or purpose. But I am an empire and every empire should be

THE CABIN

heard." She concluded magnificently powerful, her voice being replaced by a majestic
silence.

It consumed the cabin, the air, everything
even the moon seemed consumed by it.
The candles burned and illuminated desperately against the majestic silence,
fighting to maintain their own powerful-
ness. It left everyone in stupendous awe.

Chapter Five

The majestic silence morphed into plain silence, as everyone went back to contemplating his or her thoughts. The night was far from done, in the cabin, the air waited patiently until one of the many voices left conquered the silence.

Waiting and waiting, the moonlight made circles around the cabin through the windows. Waiting and waiting. Restless. Impatient. It made one circle, then a second, a third, fourth and finally on the fifth settling on a woman.

The moonlight shone brightly on the next star, the next voice.

THE CABIN

She was tall and athletic. She seemed to be in her late thirties, early forties. Her light brown hair hung straight down her back. In all, she looked strong and capable but there was a hint of delicateness in her soul. Slowly her voice traveled through the silence capturing every ones attention.

"It is hard to say good-bye. Good-bye to someone or a part of your life or especially a part of who you were. Or simply just saying good-bye can be hard. You know deep down, no matter what thing will never be the same. There is always too much room for things to change. Although, change is good, it is still a scary thought. You can't help but wonder what if this and what if that. A million questions race through you mind, like "Will I be okay?"

It is always more comforting to know worse than the unknown. At least you know what to expect and not expect from "worse", from what you know.

It is scary to take a leap into the unknown, saying good-bye to everything you know. Especially when it wasn't even your decision to make, when someone you loved pushed you into the bottomless back hole of uncertainty.

All I knew was him.

When he left me, it was early in the morning, the sun still raising. We had been talking about our future, about what would be best for us. I thought it was weird he had brought up the subject. I had always thought men weren't into talking about that kind of stuff. The future and feelings. I felt something wasn't right. He talked and talked. And the more he talked, the more I began to be under the impression that our relationship was an obstacle between him and his goals.

THE CABIN

It was all hazy and confusing. He would say I love you, I love being with you and then talk about his future and somehow I wouldn't fit in. Although he didn't say it, in those exact words, "you won't fit in" but the meaning was the same.

We never said it was over. We never talked about breaking up but when our conversation wasn't even close to being over, he stood up, walked around the table and simply kissed my forehead.

He stared straight into my eyes.

I'll never forget that moment, his eyes looking down at me. I saw our whole relationship replay itself in my mind. The moment we met, our first date, our first kiss, and the first night we moved in together and our last kiss. Everything we had done together played through my mind, in his eyes and mine.

JULES PARDO

In some deep part of me, I knew it was over.

He looked straight into my eyes and said good-bye. I tried to say good-bye too but the words couldn't come out. I was confused yet I knew everything. I think I didn't want to acknowledge it was over.

Then he left, only leaving the deafening echo of his good-bye. It resonated through the apartment for days and weeks.

I was beyond terrified as I heard the soft "click" of the door closing behind him, separating us forever.

I thought of running after him but I couldn't move. I wanted to demand an explanation. I wanted to ask him if it was really happening or if I were going crazy and making everything up. I didn't know what to do.

I contemplated my choices. What could I do? Go look for him or never think of him

THE CABIN

again. Beg for his love or keep whatever was left of my pride. Maybe move somewhere or find a rebound guy or something. Or maybe pretend like our conversation never happened and wait for him... or etc....

Through the tears I cried, I waited for him every day. I cried until one day, I was completely dry that nothing could come out. The pain was still unbearable. I still clung hard onto what he had left, onto the life we had led together. I did everything as if he was coming back, as though he never left. In the mornings, I made his coffee with cream and sugar and scrambled eggs with peanut butter toast, just how he liked it.

I was in denial...

I saw him again. I saw him waiting alone outside a store, looking down at his phone. I half yelled his name and he looked up. I remember he was shocked to see me. Eyes wide and all. I ran up to him and hugged him like I was never letting go. Which I wouldn't have if he hadn't gently pushed me back and introduce me to his pregnant wife who had stepped out of the store. He said good-bye and left once again. Only this time, hand in hand with his pregnant wife while I stood dumbfounded on the sidewalk.

I was speechless.

I knew in that second I had to let go. I had to say good-bye. To accept he had let go and moved on. It had been little more than a year he had left. I had to say good-bye.

Whatever we had, had been just that. Nothing more.

Have you ever loved someone so much it became who you are?" She asked looking around, searching in his or her eyes. "I loved him like that. I had become the woman who he wanted. I was just not the woman for him...

THE CABIN

My identity had been him. Who was I now? I thought of myself ugly and inferior. I thought I wasn't good enough for him. I wonder would I ever be good enough for anyone. My self-esteem really hit rock bottom.

On top of all that, I was scared, terrified to move on, to change and ultimately say good-bye. I won't lie, it took me some time, more than I care to admit now, to move on but eventually I did. I became my own woman. I became happy without the need to have a man. I became very happy and free. My self-esteem restored.

But the memory of him, of us still hurts. On a night like this, I can't help but think of him, of who I used to be. He did not die but to me when he left, it felt like a violent death. I lost everything I had known, everything I wanted and loved. I mourned the death of our unforgiving love.

JULES PARDO

I still think of him sometimes, fleeting thoughts. I know he moved on and so I have, but I wonder if he sometimes thinks of me or remembers our love..." She paused thoughtful.

"Today I couldn't be happier. Change is good. Never forget the future is better in its own way. Accept it and embrace it. It is okay to feel pain, to feel lost and scared. Feel it and once in a while remember it. We have to say good-bye to the moment but never to the memory," she said with a soft glowing smiling. She had a positive energy surrounding her but deep in her eyes laid pain.

Close by her, a young woman held the same pain in her hazel eyes. She regarded the woman thoughtfully, her brown eyebrows furring in concentration. She was in her very early twenties, maybe twenty or

THE CABIN

twenty-one. She could not be more than twenty-three, maximum.

She sat in the small circle of three chairs. The other chairs were occupied by young women who were around her age. They had mostly likely seated together because they would be more comfortable around other women their own age. Even though they were all physically different, they all held a certain similarity, which unified them.

A couple of candles stood in the middles of their circle. She stared into the flames as she though, as she spoke. The flames danced as her breath hit them. They danced to her voice. Concentrating on the flames, after a couple of minutes she said, "I used to love who I was. I liked how I looked. Well, in all honesty, I didn't care how I looked or acted, it wasn't important when I was little. But before, I use to love myself.

JULES PARDO

Now… Every morning, I look at myself in the mirror. And every single morning, I hate whom I see. I hate my hair, my skin, my body. I especially hate my body shape. I just hate it. It's just not right. Clothes don't look right on me….

I'm not content with who I am and how I look.

I feel hopeless and as if, I am drowning in a sea of self-hatred.

I try talking about it but they always say the same thing "You are gorgeous the way you are", "It's okay to have curves" and my favorite "Real men love curves."

It might be true "Real men love curves" but all I see is men settle down with skinny women. I see men drool over tall and slim models in magazines.

I get so confused.

THE CABIN

Then they say, "You are slightly over-weight." Well actually, they say it more diplomatically you know like "maybe you should think about joining a gym" or they say "I think you should order a salad" while their gaze drops to my stomach.

I lose weight and everything is all right for a while. I get nice compliments. I feel better about myself and I am happy but it never lasts. I become obsessed with how I want my body to look and on most days I feel as fat as I used to be, sometimes even fatter. I know I'm not but I feel like I am. And then I hate myself for sacrificing some foods and time to look just right when, at the end of the day, I feel as if I am the fattest woman alive.

At the end of the day, I am still not happy with whom I am.

Then they say, "Skinny women aren't as pretty as women with curves" and "women with curves are way better" Then somehow I end up being judge for having lost weight. They tell me I shouldn't have let the superficial idea of beauty, which the media creates, change who I am. And they ask me accusingly why I am wasting my time obsessing about my weight and image.

They say, "Women are beautiful the way they are, especially curvy women." Then I see men drool over curvy actresses and models with big boobs, big butt or both. I put back on some weight, just enough to achieve sizable curves and I get hated on. I can't get natural curves without gaining fat in my arms, things and belly.

They ask me disgusted "Why don't you take care of yourself? Men like women who take care of themselves"

I get hated on, ignored and judged.

So, I eat more and more, I gain more weight until one morning, I can't stand the sight of myself anymore and I begin to lose weight. I lose weight again and people judge me for being skinny, for losing my curves, for having lost weight to be skinny.

It's unfair.

I see some women who become skinny and they don't get judged but that's because since the beginning, they always claimed they are doing it to be healthy. So then, everyone respects them and supports them.

They become inspirational.

But I think they just want to be skinny like me. I think the only difference is, they say, "I want to be healthy" while I straight out say "I want to be skinny."

Anyways since when did having a completely, unachievable flat stomach become the image of healthiness? I ask myself that every time I see one of those women go from like a size ten to a two, with a complete flat stomach.

A size six is healthy, no?

It probably is but it doesn't feel beautiful. Size zero up to 2 are beautiful sizes apparently. Sizes, which give you confidence. You are the same size as a model. Whoohooo!" She said faking enthusiasm. "I could be the same size as a model but I will never be as pretty as them. It is not in my gene pool.

You know how they always ask, "Does size matter"?

You want to know the answer?

For women size matters. A lot. But don't tell anyone. No woman would actually want to admit it. A size zero, a size four, a size ten, it all matters. What sizes their friends wear, matters. What sizes celebrities wear, matters.

Measurements matter...

THE CABIN

You know what also matters? Your word choice to express how you want your body to look like.

The word "healthy" makes everything okay. You know, acceptable.

No matter what you do, don't say "I want to be skinny" it is a taboo. I said it and it was a taboo but when I put the weight back on, it was another taboo.

Taboo after taboo. Skinny after fat, fat after skinny. Judgment after judgment. Gaining after losing, losing after gaining. Never perfect, never happy, never looking right and never finding the perfect way to please men completely.

It's an endless circle.

I am tired and exhausted.

I can't stand the sight of myself.

I detest going out, especially in summer.

Nothing is ever right. My hair is uncooperative. My outfits unflattering and out of style. My body and skin are covered with imperfections.

I am tired of this circle..." she finished saying drained with unbearable sadness lodged in her throat. Still staring intently into the candle flames, her eyes clouded with more pain and sorrow. The dark circles under her eyes became even darker as she fell deeper and deeper into her thoughts.

Interrupting her thoughts, the woman in front of her, to her right said looking also into the flames, "I understand what you mean." She looked up from the flames as everyone else turned to look at her. The flames moved more as her voice hit them, like an angry dance instead of the moderate sway they had danced to the other woman's voice.

"Every day I see models and actresses in all their perfection and glory, while I feel completely worthless. I try to comfort my-self by saying it is all Photoshop but then when I go out, I see every woman possess something I don't. They all have that per-fect something. They are all perfect... well not perfect completely, they just have that little something I would love to have to be perfect...

The thing is, the second I realize she has something I want, whether it's her hair, skin or body (You know like legs, butt, boobs, flat belly, arm or small waist or whatever.) In that, second I hate them. I..." she paused searing for the perfect word "I just hate them," she said as-a-matter-of-factly and simply. "I hate them with all my being. All I want in that second is for them to be miser-able. I just want them to suffer. Somehow, I find it makes me feel better when I see them suffer. I mean they can't have perfection and happiness. It wouldn't be fair. They can't have everything.

Only I can.

I know you might think I am cruel or whatever but I don't care. I speak the truth. It is something I can't control. And it's not only with women physically, I mean whenever another woman is doing something, anything, better than me I just need to… to… destroy them… yeah… destroy… destroy describes it nicely…" she nodded satisfied.

"The worst part is the smart ones barely know how to dress or have you ever noticed they act really weird.

It's quite sad," she said faking sadness. "But whatever…

In all honesty, whatever this is, it rules my life.

I want to be the only one who is more perfect than models and actresses. I want to be

THE CABIN

the only one who succeeds. Many call it "jealousy" or whatever but it's not. I know the difference. Whatever this is, it's not my problem. It's just that there is always someone out there who has a better body than me with perfect boobs and butt and waist. Or someone smarter, more talented and everything than me. And it just infuriates me so much. If they have a boyfriend too.... It takes everything I have not too literally destroy them. They aren't perfect and they have a boyfriend? I mean what's that all about?

Anyways I am perfect, I mean look at me." She laughed bitterly and smugly. Confusion knit everyone's brows together.

"So anyways, that's all," she said and became silent.

Her silence put uncomfortable the others. It didn't help that she had a sour expression with her lips pursed and her eyes faintly squinted. She had both arms and legs crossed tightly. It was clear she was furious.

Silence stretched out for a couple of minutes, uncomfortably. No one was able to escape to his or her thoughts or anything as her silence made them feel they should stay alert. Her silence imprisoned them, although more the other women than the men.

All the women seemed uneasy and some slightly scared. Something about her had set them into submission. Or maybe it was more self-preservation than submission or anything else. It must have been how her stare shifted between murderous and passive aggressive. She was like a ticking bomb. At any moment, she might explode the slightest touch of a breath.

No women found comfort in the situation, the possibility.

THE CABIN

She hadn't threatened them but they knew if they talked, commented, or drew any type of attention to them, they could be destroyed.

Self-preservation always wins, no matter how big or small the situation might be.

The third young woman in the circle had wanted to talk. She had wanted to talk after the first women had spoken but hadn't had the courage to speak. During the second woman's speech, she built her courage but was beaten by the last woman who had spoken. During the last woman's speech, she had rebuilt up her courage to speak once again but know she seemed unsure if she should speak at all.

Her eyes betrayed her inner battle.

To talk or not to talk.

It seems as if she was confused and scared. She opened her mouth then quickly shut it. Her brown eyes surveyed the room terrified and she cringed into her seat as if she had done something wrong and was waiting to be punished.

After looking around a second time, her body relaxed in unison with her eyes. She took a deep breath and opened her mouth to speak but once again shut it quickly. She did this three times before taking one long deep breath and exhaling loudly.

Those around her turned to stare at her, eyebrows raised in astonishment. They were surprised there was someone there. They had overlooked her.

An invisible soul.

She looked at them taking a smaller, quicker deep breath, and turned her gaze to her hands in her lap, where she fidgeted and played with her figures, and said in a small voice, which made the flames dance soft gentle dance, "I feel worthless too." Her voice was barely above a whisper.

THE CABIN

"Every day I feel worthless. I wish I were someone else. I wish I looked different. I wish... I wish he would love me for me. Every day I spend my time wishing. I wish I were good enough for him. I wish I could become who he wants me to be. I want to make him happy.

Every day he tells me I am ugly... and he is right, I am. I know I am. He says I'm too fat, that I don't have enough boobs or ass and I don't know how to dress. He also tells me constantly how lucky I am to be with him. I am lucky to be with him. He could easily be with a tall, fit and drop, dead gorgeous blond, as he reminds me every day. But instead, he is with me.

... I sometimes feel as if I shouldn't be with him but I love him. I will do anything I can to make him happy. I try to dress better and sometimes that helps but whenever I try to copy one of the sexy girls on the posters we have in our bedroom, which he is always staring at, he gets so mad. He yells at me that I am whore, a worthless whore and then he hits me.

He hits me often. Maybe every other day. It is rarely ever hard and he mostly leaves small marks. But I don't mind because it makes him happy. I know it does because he always has a smile threatening to appear on his lips when he hits me and he always seems content after he beats me or leaves me lying on the floor. He especially loves it when I try to resist or when I try not to scream. It makes him very happy and I want him to be happy.

It's my job to make him happy.

He tells me that's my only purpose in life because he loves me and no one else does. Not even my family. He always says, especially my family doesn't love me. He reminds me of all the wrong they have done to me and says it prove they have never loved and never will but he loves me. He tells me if I want to make sure I am loved, I have to make him happy because he will love me.

I want to be loved. If he doesn't love me then who will?

I sometimes..." she became quiet and thoughtful abruptly. Her eyebrows inclining together. Seconds passed by turning into minutes, as she was lost in the sea of her thoughts. Her brown eyes stared at the flames but her gaze was covered with a muddy screen of emotions.

Everyone still paid attention to her. In particular, the young man, who had spoken earlier in the night about wanting to find the woman who would be able to see past his outbursts. He stared at the young woman as if she were a rare diamond. His eyes shown with concern for her. As she had talked, he had inched closer and closer to her from his seat until his bottom was barely touching the chair. Even from far away, his posture was somehow protective of her.

Even though everyone had developed, a protective stance regarding her, his over-powered them all. Even the woman who spoke before her turned her body protec-tively towards her. She still gave the other young woman envious stares every now and then but the innocence her neighbor exuded was like a small hurt animal in need of help.

But Innocence is lost in the first breath the baby takes and for the years to come is con-fused with ignorance. In the first breath, the baby breathes in all that the world has to offer, happiness and sufferings, uncer-tainties with the only certainty of death. In the first breath, the baby is filled with the

THE CABIN

knowledge of the world, of the air, of all the history and energy. No wonder they cry for their dear life shortly after. What a world they have to live in now.

It's a shame though, with time that knowledge is lost and only gained back in the last years of life. Unless they were wise enough to never let go of that first breath. To always cherish it, to never actually grow up and leave their childlike thinking behind in the treasure box of memories.

They awaited for her to finish her sentence or speak. They wanted more.

She exhaled with sorrow, turned her gaze back to her lap, and twisted her figures repeatedly as her delicate voice traveled through the silence.

"I wish I could look like the dream woman he wishes I were. Or, at the very least, look like one of the women he stares at when we go out or flirts with in front of me.

JULES PARDO

I wish I were enough for him.

He shows me pictures of women and asks me angrily "Why can't you be like them?", "Why do you have to be so ugly?"

When he leaves, I spend hours looking at the pictures. I put them on the full-length mirror in our room and I stare at the pictures then back at myself and back and forth. I try to find out what they have that I don't. They have everything, beauty and they must be intelligent too. They are the whole package, while I am not. I am worthless like he says...

But I love him so much. I try really hard to be the perfect girlfriend for him.

He says I have an ugly voice. He... he... he... he hates it when I talk" her voice broke at the end. She looked frighten, as if she committed an unforgivable crime. She cringed into her seat becoming smaller, trying to protect herself. She looked up from her lap, eyes wide in terror.

She looked around at the people in the cabin, realizing no one would hit her, she quickly pleaded, "Please don't tell him any-thing. He is a very private man. It's one of the qualities I love about him. I don't know what possessed me to talk. I..." The words tumbled rapidly out of her lips, out of fear. It was impossible not to share what the soul most wanted to tell when it was all it could do, all it could do to remain sane on such a night.

In her moment of panic, she had forgot-ten, she was in a room with strangers. Strangers who did not know him.

She became quiet and thoughtful.

After a couple of seconds, she said, "He al-ways means well and he is a great guy. I mean he loves me after all even though I am not enough for him. If he didn't love me, he would be with someone better than me. I know he loves me and I love him." Her words were spoken more robotically than with any emotion now. "I love him so much," she said unsure, becoming quiet once more.

Everyone was confused. Why be with someone who treats her like that? Why? No one quite understood. It is always complex situation when a woman loves and is devoted to the man who mistreats her.

There is no arguing with them, they cannot be convinced. For them, their lovers do no wrong. Trying to help some of them is a dead end. Some women will go back to their beloved. It's the same love as a woman, who awaits for her beloved husband too return from war. The same love as a dog who will always be loyal to his master.

Sometimes the women are too scared to leave because they know the man will

THE CABIN

haunt them down and hurt them even more than before and ultimately his manipulation will lead her back into the black room of torture, with one window of hope that someday she might be free.

Sometimes it is the man. No matter how cruel he is, no matter how many times he tells her he hates her or he doesn't want her, he will never let her go because she is his. She is his forever because he needs her. Because he is sick with an illness, which is too often over, looked by society.

Lack of love. Too much aggressively. Feelings of inferiority.

Symptoms of his illness, which he takes out on her because what will she do? He has the power. And in a twisted way, he loves her.

"I love him," she said more to herself than anyone else but her voice rang with uncertainty. She nodded to herself trying to convince herself. But it was clear, now having everything laid out for her by her soul. She couldn't hide from the truth. Words weren't enough for her now because she had to confront the truth. Whether she wanted or not, she had to acknowledge whatever she had with him was not what she thought it was and maybe deep down she wasn't in love with him as the automatic words she spoke had indicated.

She sat frowning in confusion and perplexity.

Everyone turned back to contemplating his or her thoughts as well. Always so much to ponder about.

Four women.

One older and wiser but still burden with pain. A pain three young women could, in their own way, identify themselves with. Age was just a number, insignificant to pain.

THE CABIN

Wisdom was irrelevant to pain. Pain stuck whenever, wherever and however it wanted.

Three women.

Three women. Three different situations and yet all of them desire to be someone else. They hate their bodies and who they are. They are confused and hurt. The world tells them they are capable strong women. Then the world picks at their insecurities to gain power over them while destroying their strength.

Three women who have never met one another and yet they shared the same pain. It would not be surprising if all women felt or have felt the same way once in their life.

Is it a rite of passage? Maybe to grow or is it just a painful reminder to accept who they are?

Body, hair, skin, clothes, it all comes down to beauty.

JULES PARDO

Why is beauty so important?

Three women who represented the modern woman who instead of being controlled by tradition and inferiority, they are controlled by beauty. It dictated their lives. It controls them making them believe it is the new way of life. How it is meant to be. How it's always been.

Maybe that is why it is so important.

But with beauty comes insecurities, feelings of worthlessness, a gut-wrenching pain consuming their hearts.

Beauty holds the power men once had on women. Beauty is the power women could have but they let it dominate them while they believe they have the power.

Three women who can find comfort in one another, who belong to the same pain, a feeling, an emotion stronger than them.

Three women who could be friends.

THE CABIN

They could be best friends. They could unite and battle against the new "tradition."

But they will compare themselves with one another, tinting any kind of relationship with a certain dishonesty. A certain barrier, forbidding them to be truly close.

Could they be honest with one another? Could they ever stop comparing themselves with others? Is comparing themselves in their blood now forever? Could they one morning wake up and love themselves and not feel threatened by other each or their own fears? Is that the hope of the future for women? To hope they will not compare themselves to each other? Or are women content the way it is and always has been? Three women who think they are not enough and ugly but who, in their own way, are gorgeous. They are unique like every other woman on earth. Like all women, they are delicately strong flower filled with wisdom, life, love, power strength and un-deniable beauty.

There is always hope for them to realize their beauty and to free themselves from self-torture and emotional harm they inflict on their spirits.

Chapter Six

Silence settled effortlessly in the cabin. The once deafening silence was now dull. But its dullness captured and trapped everyone's souls into absolute stillness.

Minds could only think.

They could only be lost in the universe of their thoughts.

Time became truly immeasurable.

The atmosphere began transforming itself into a fog of uncertainty, forcing every soul to do the same. It spread through the cabin, feeding on their doubts. It spread through the cabin making their doubts grow into their own beings.

JULES PARDO

The dullness of the silence now hung above their heads like clouds threatening to pour unstoppable, thick tears of doubt. Like acid rain, waiting to burn them with uncertainty.

Breaths came out quicker and fearful.

Eyes held all the vagueness of the past, all the incertitude of the future with anguish.

After minutes of immeasurable time, a very young man with exquisite deep blue eyes and dark hair said out of the blue "I dream… I hope …. But will it ever be enough?

Doubts torturously and ever so slowly kill my confidence that one day I will achieve my dreams. Do I have what it takes? Am I destined for those dreams or shall they forever be just dreams.

Theses doubts make me nostalgic for a time I long. A time I have only lived in my imagination. In my imagination where it is so perfect, I wonder if it is "too good to be true". It is so perfect it hurts.

THE CABIN

I am nostalgic because I lived it once in my mind and my doubts are like the time slowly passing by, leaving my dream in the grand ocean of the past. I am drowning in nostalgia, desperately trying to grasp my dreams to make them a reality.

I feel my dreams… my hopes slip through my fingers into the water of my past, leaving me empty-handed only with a few drops of water reminding I could have had them. I could have fulfilled my dreams.

But my doubts…

I feel as though my doubts have built a brick wall around my heart. I feel as if I have lost the war before it began, before it was even declared.

I can feel my heart frantically trying to break down the brick wall but is it strong enough? Am I strong enough?" He asked in whisper.

"Doubts kill your heart's spirit first and then ever so slowly ends with your soul. I fear the day my soul will take its last breath, leaving me with a soulless body roaming the streets, living a so-called life.

I fear the day I will fear more than dream. And my dreams will excise it to exist...

Do I have what it takes? Am I strong enough? Will I be able succeed? I'm I destined for it?

I must be strong. I have to be. I want my dreams to be true no matter what. It may not be a need but neither is it a simple desire. It's something I feel that comes from the bottom of my being. It pushes me to grab on tightly to my dreams and hopes and never let go. Even though at times it seems impossible to grasp water.

I can't let go. I won't let go.

I can't let doubts rule my life. I have to be the king of the sea and ruler of my dreams and hopes.

I dream... I hope it will be make me strong enough to succeed." He finished saying hopeful. He relaxed into his seat, looking around the cabin.

He met her eyes.

THE CABIN

She stared back his stunning blue eyes. She gazed at his handsome face searching while his gaze ran all over her body searching too. Their eyes met again. No electricity passed through them. His eyes flirted with her, her eyes with his but they felt nothing. No sparks. No excitement.

Absolutely nothing passed between them.

She smiled apologetic and he smiled back knowingly. He shrugged his broad shoulders as in saying "Hey we can't always be everyone's cup of tea." And winked at her. She giggled inaudibly.

The silence began settling around the cabin. But it was disrupted by her soft-spoken voice.

"Sometimes I feel as if my life was already written for me. As if I am a mere actor robotically saying every line and now and then has the power to change a few words but never the meaning of the original...

I must always act a certain way. I must always be proper or not be at all.

I must follow the rules.

JULES PARDO

Why do I do this? When I was little, I asked myself but I figured along the road, it was because the people I love with all my heart tell me to do so.

I wonder what my life would have been if I had been born in a different family. Who would I be? Would I be the same person? Would I even be alive? What would my life be like?" She paused contemplating her thoughts.

"I hate to admit it but I love option and absolutely hate choosing. I didn't want to chose when I was younger and I don't want to choose now. There are too many options, too many paths, too many different possibilities.

I am at a multiple crossroad.

And for once I will choose my own path. But I don't know which one to choose. It's too much.

What if I make the wrong decision?

My parents know me best. They know what is best for me. I guess that's why I always let them chose. However, I know

THE CABIN

whatever path I choose now on my own, tears will be shed and feelings will get hurt. I know they will be hurt because the outcome may not be what they desired. It hurts me to know I will hurt the ones I love most but I have to choose this time on my own. I owe myself that much. I have to know if I can be a strong and independent woman.

No matter the path I choose, it will be the biggest change I have ever had. It's a scary thought. It's too much to think about. Too many possibilities and consequences." She became quiet, her mind getting lost in her thoughts. A strand of brown hair with blond highlights fell on her shoulder from her loose ponytail.

The candles illuminated her polished features as she lifted a little her chin and said determinedly "But I will choose nevertheless. I have to choose because..." she breathed in a deep steadying breath.

"Because I have always felt like I must watch my every action, my every words utter by my lips. Even my breathing because if I did it wrong, it would make them unhappy. I must be careful. Very careful as if I were walking on a delicate layer of thin glass. One misstep and it all shutters into a million pieces cutting everyone around me and making me bleed." She paused again.

"More than proving to myself I can be a strong, independent woman, I need to prove I am not going crazy.

I always feel as though I am on the verge of going insane. Just one slip and next thing I'll know I will be in an asylum. I try to control my emotions. I train hard to master every single emotion I possess. But I sometimes feel any second they will consume me and turn me senseless.

I have to be composed for the sakes of others. I really hate when I let an emotion get the better of me, no matter if it's happiness or anger or sadness, it changes everything in a second. I think I feel/show my

THE CABIN

emotions to strongly and afterwards I feel like the lowest human being alive.

If I want happiness for others, shall I suffer?

I know I do. I know I must put my feelings aside and do things for others. I must give up my dreams; give up my happiness for them. I must be selfless" she laughed humorously.

"I wish I could be selfless, truly selfless but in all honestly I think I might be one of the world's most selfish person, who as ever lived. I spend all day thinking about myself.

In theory being selfless sounds good but in practice I don't think I have what it takes. I love me too much I guess or whatever thing I possess which makes people unable to be selfless.

Although I am trained to make sure everyone believes I am selfless. And I do foul most people but I can't tonight. It felt wrong when I tried.

I need to choose my own path to prove I am not going crazy. I need to choose my own path because I want to be free and happy. I need to choose my own path because I need to become who I am and not who I should.

But I still have concerns.

They taught me well...."She said half bitterly half lovingly. "I wish I didn't care about them. It would make everything so much easier. But they taught me well and in some deep part of me I have concerns that I might hurt them. But will it stop me? Probably not.

I do love them and want to make everyone happy including myself. And no matter which path I choose, I will be on their side however I can. I have given them my best and always will. I just hope they will understand.

I need something else.

The life I lead does not fulfill me the way I wish.

I want to be free.

They will understand if they love me right? She asked a little worried. Then a flash of determination shone in her eyes as she said "it doesn't matter. I will choose what will be best for me."

No argument. No doubt. No fear.

She relaxed her poster like a solider being told "at ease".

Close by the door, a woman sat with her back to a window, looking at her. She studied her for a couple of seconds and said "I know how you feel. Sort of. About making choices I mean.

I had to make a choice but in instead I ran away.

Literally.

I got scared and ran away from everything. I convinced myself over the years I made the right decision. But what if I hadn't ran away. What if I would have had the courage? If I had the courage back then would it have changed things? If I had faith everything would be better, would it have mattered?

I will never know." Her eyebrow furred in concentration. She sighed.

JULES PARDO

"After I ran away, it seemed easy to run away when things got hard to deal with. I ran away from every problem I couldn't handle or didn't want to handle.

I know, I know" she said putting her hands in the air in surrender. "It's a coward's way out but the anguish of thinking how to deal with everything was so overwhelming.

My heart beating at a thousand miles an hour. I could hardly breathe. My palm would turn dead cold and sweaty. My thoughts tumbled into one another, never making sense, always incoherent and never helping me.

The only thoughts that ever seemed to make sense was run away.

I regret running away the first time.

A few days ago, I was talking with my mother on the phone, who, as usual was filling me in on the latest gossip of our little town. To be honest, I was barely paying attention to what she was saying until she repeated twice the same sentence, emphasizing his name dramatically.

THE CABIN

"He is getting married," I repeated in disbelieve.

It hit me so hard. It crushed me into a small ball in the corner of my kitchen. I trembled as each emotion hit me. It was like someone was throwing big, heavy bricks of what could have been at me.

I was supposed to marry him. We were supposed to live happily ever after but... but we weren't right for each other. Or maybe we were. I don't know.

A few short weeks after he proposed, I began feeling alone. When I was with him I felt utterly alone. I loved him but for weeks I got a nagging feeling I was making a mistake. I kept wondering what if this and what if that.

As I began the wedding preparation, it became too much.

I was the definition of unhappy.

I tried talking to him but either he was busy or I would chicken out. At the end I panicked and took off, without the slightest explanation.

JULES PARDO

I blamed him for so many years because it seemed better than blaming myself. I blamed him for everything, especially for my running away. Somehow I was convinced it was his fault. I know it is not his fault. He never forced me or hinted that I should run away. He even tried to come after me…" she paused deep in thought. Many emotions burned in her eyes. Her mouth curved faintly downward as she thought.

"In a way, I am glad is getting married but I also feel betrayed, you know. I think deep down I hope he would wait for me. Wait until I realized what a horrible mistake I had made and would forgive and take me back. He had promised me he would always love me no matter what. I guess I really believed in the "no matter what" part. And I think he forgot to mention an expiration date on his love." She said accusingly.

"I know…" she said putting her hands in the air in surrender once again. "I know, I know… I am not being fair to him but I am

THE CABIN

angry. He gets to have the life I have always dreamed, in the town I love while I have to dream up a new dream in someplace else. And pretend it's what I have wanted since I was little, my childhood dream.

I can't go back and start a life there. My pride won't let me" she took a deep breath and said thoughtfully

"I have been wondering these past few days what my life would have been if we had gotten married.

I think by now we would have had children. I think we would have been real happy if I hadn't been so complex.

I regret not marrying him. He is that type of man who makes a wonderful husband. He's got a little bit of everything in him. And I gave that up... That wonderful husband...

I am tired of looking for my "perfect one."

Right now I would much rather dwell on what could have been, then think of the possible ways I could mess things up in the future, leading me to run away again.

JULES PARDO

What if I had been completely happy with him?" She asked looking around but no one answered.

What could they answer her?

She didn't press the issue further. Instead she lowered herself on her seat until her neck was on the edge of the back of the seat. She extended her legs in front of her, closing her eyes and began to taking long deep breathes. Her lean body trembled softly every now and then.

Some people looked at her trying to understand the situation. Did she still love him or is it simply the idea she could have been married she wanted?

Others regarded her with compassion.

The rest were simply thoughtful.

Behind her, through the windows, the moon was high in the sky. The sky was cleared of stars and clouds. The night still calm as ever.

A few people stared out the window from their seats. Snowflakes cover delicately the bottom edge of each window. The windows

THE CABIN

showed a never changing scenery, it was as if someone had glued a powerful photography worth a million words on the windows; Snow until the end of the horizon and where the horizon finished black sky shot up in the empty air, intimidating with all its simplicity.

All there was, was snow surrounding them. There was so much snow, that even if they could find someway to open the doors, there was nothing near and it would take days to shovel the snow and walk to the nearest town.

They were snowed into a cabin in the middle of nowhere.

There was a possibility they would all die there. Whatever life they had lead, this could be the end for them.

Two, three stared out the windows hopeless and defeated.

Chapter Seven

With a light cloud of uncertainty still roaming through the cabin, a young handsome man sat motionless, deep in thought. He had been one of those who had been staring out the window at what seemed to be their fate. He had dark brown eyes and brown hair. All his features were very masculine like his broad shoulders.

He sat staring at the floor, his eyes flickering from side to side quickly, as if he were watching intently the ball of an animated Ping-Pong match.

One side, then the other. Back and forth.

THE CABIN

His eyebrows smashed into each other in concentration. His eyes deep in consternation. His posture revealed a hint of frustration as he clasped his large hands together.

He exhaled loudly relaxing his large tense body, letting his shoulders fall.

Into the night's silence, he said, "The past is the past.

It is full of memories. It is our only prove we have existed.

We will always carry it with us.

It is the one thing we know for sure will never change. No matter how much we sometimes wish we could. It can never be forgotten. It is a part of whom we are and it lets us grow. The past was the future we feared so much. The unknown became known.

It sometimes is the only thing we truly own, along with our thoughts. No one can take our past or our thoughts away from us. It belongs to us.

We can sometimes even rely on the past to bring us comfort when times are hard. We can clutch on to it and let it hug us with its reassurance when we feel lost. But it is sometimes the one thing we most desperately need to let go but simply can't because it is a part of you, because in hard times you could rely on it, because it was there for you. Because, it taught you things no schools or any education could ever teach. Because in the end, the past is you.

I am grateful for my past but I wonder if I had done things differently would I be in a better place? I am happy, really I am. But there is something in me that isn't quite satisfied.

THE CABIN

I try finding different ways to be truly complete. And whenever I find that something that was missing, I feel my past stop me from moving forward, from enjoying the moment. It paralyses me. And that infuriates me.

I want to put my past into a vault, lock it forever, and store it in the back of my mind, in a black hole of forgotten things.

I have...,"He grunted with a mixture of frustration and disgust. Closed his eyes and turned his head to the side and through slightly clenched teeth, he said "I have become afraid...

I don't know if I can trust people.

I am afraid that I'll make the wrong decision and not end up where I would belong or where I would be happy and complete. I am afraid I'll get hurt...

I hope my future will be everything I have dreamed. I hope I will find true happiness. I know some people say you cannot find happiness because it is something, which has to be searched from within. It's true but it is not true happiness. I think you also need to find it in a place or person for it to be completely true happiness. You would have the happiness from within but also your surroundings would help.

Day after day being happy. It would be a dream come true."

He became quiet, thoughtful. Seconds passed by and people began to wonder if he had finished but they could sense he wasn't done. His mind had to ponder on his thoughts.

More seconds passed by.

Finally, he spoke once more.

"To be honest, I think finding happiness elsewhere is an excuse. Don't get me wrong, I do believe in what I said… It's just… that in my mind I pin all my hopes on

THE CABIN

finding happiness elsewhere because I don't want to search within me.

My past always takes hold of my thoughts and dictates my mind.

Memories of happiness. Memories of dark times.

It becomes like pouring black and white paint into a bowl then stirring everything. Memories of happiness swirls with dark memories, until everything is a dull depressing gray. I become cynical and dark. Distrusting of people. Bitter and resentful. Only seeing the negative in everything.

I hate it.

Life is always much more fun when I am happy. Everything seems to fall into place. All my problems don't affect me as much and I can think clearly." He paused.

"I hope I will find true happiness. And when I do, I vow to only look forward to all the possibilities of the future and not dwell on the past. Not let the past cast shadows of distrust on my life.

I will be happy," he said softly. His face glowed with hope. Whatever his plan was to achieve happiness, it was now heavily tinted with hope and determination.

On the other side of the room, across from him, a young woman with light brown hair stared at the man with admiration.

She looked down at the floor and became very thoughtful. She was around the same age as the young handsome man, maybe a bit younger mid-twenties. She had dark passionate eyes, which sparkled with emotions. In candlelight, her subtle features were lit almost angelically.

A few minutes went by in complete silence, then suddenly the young woman said "Have you ever wonder how different your life would be if you took a left turn instead of a right? Would you be the same person you are now? Would you be friends with the same type of people?

I wonder everyday... there are days where I feel like I have made all the right decisions... but most days... I wonder... I don't know... how different things might be... if I... I... or... I..." she exhaled, letting go the breath she had held since she began mumbling.

She took a deep breath and said, "I dwell on the past and then the future and back to the past and again to the future. Kind of like you," she said in a sweet soft voice, looking at the young handsome man who had spoken before her.

Their eyes met. In a nanosecond, connection went between them locking their souls as one. Her dark brown eyes sparkled as his shined. He gave her a dazzling smile and she smiled back delighted, her cheeks turning pinker. She broke eye contact first, look-ing down at her hands in her lap. Still smil-ing, she delicately shook her head with amused disbelieve.

"Uh..."she said biting her bottom lip.

"I believe in there are no such things as bad decisions. Some decisions you make are meant to be lessons like they say. You had to learn something from it to be able to grow as a person, to move on from a certain phase of your life... But I looked around me and I feel out of place. I feel as if I don't belong here. I can't see what I need to learn from this.

I don't understand...

I really do wonder if I made the right de-cision to make a right turn instead of a left, if you know what I mean. If I had taken a left turn, would I feel like I belong wher-ever I might have ended? Would I feel like I am in the right place?

THE CABIN

I wonder if I am going through a phase where I am changing my lifestyle and beliefs and that's why I feel like I don't fit in. Or is it because I realized who I am and it doesn't fit in with whom I surround myself with? Or maybe I just never fit in and now I finally realized it?

… I wonder if it's all in my head…. You know… That I made myself believe I don't fit in because I am not happy, because it's not how I imagined I would end up like. I know the mind can be powerful, it dictates our action, our feelings. It makes us believe we are happy when we are not.

I know by experience.

It makes us believe so many things and I wonder if it's my mind, which makes me believe I don't belong here.

But I know it's not my mind.

JULES PARDO

The feeling I get comes from the very core of my existence. It is always constant, always the same, never changing and never fading.

It makes me wonder if I should set out on a journey to find the perfect place where I belong, where I can be happy and I can be myself. A place where all my doubts on making the right decision vanish because in my mind, in my gut, I will know I have found the perfect place for me" she said happily.

The young handsome man's eyes never left her face from the moment he laid eyes on her. He regarded her with undisputable affection as she spoke. When she finished speaking, her lips began turning into a smile but as her gaze caught his, she lost her breath. His eyes were shinning with warmth as his smile held all the certainty, all the charm in the world.

THE CABIN

"You should go on that journey and I should join you. We can help each other out. I'll help you find the place where you'll belong perfectly and you can help me find happiness. What do you say? We leave in the morning, yes?" he said with a playful touch of seduction and confidence.

She looked as if what the man said wasn't a big deal but her eyes glittered like a million stars in the sky, giving her away. She pursed her lips looking upward, tapping her finger on her chin, thinking it over playfully. She looked up from her lashes.

"I think we have a deal," she said flirtatiously and laughed lightly, making the million stars in her eyes dance.

"Perfect" he said smiling, his bright, dark eyes sparkling with delight. Maybe more than he cared to show.

The way they stared at each other smiling, left no doubt that at the very least, they found each other attractive and/or interesting. But it was more like love at first sight. It was a true feeling of love, something real, something more than attraction and everyone could feel it. A connection of two bare souls uniting as one. They seemed to radiate light around them as if they were glowing with love.

An old man with dirty ripped clothes sat in right the center of the cabin. He looked at the man and woman exchange looks of a thousand words. He studied them intently for a couple of minutes.

He had a bushy salt and pepper beard with white hair. And he was dirty. Every inch of him was covered in filth. He was also very, very old, his eyes heavily wrinkled by life.

He was a homeless man, traveling through towns.

THE CABIN

The moonlight shone brightly on him from every window. Eight spotlights on him. He studied briefly the new couple once more then he stared into nothingness with his eyes far away into the past. His raspy old voice carried out through the cabin caressing everyone.

"The memory of her is a part of me as is my heart. I need it to continue on.

She was the type of person you came across once in a lifetime. She was the only person who was ever honest with me, who understood me and completed my life. She accepted who I was without any judgment.

I loved her like there was no tomorrow. We loved with our hearts and nothing more." He laughed. "Well we didn't have anything else to give but our hearts. We were poor as one could be but we didn't care. As long as we were together, the rest didn't matter.

JULES PARDO

The moment we became one, we realized we had more than the richest of people.

We had true love.

Our souls fit perfectly together like two puzzle pieces. Our bodies were nurtured with love and joy. Our love was our home. It was where we could find refuge and safety.

While everyone else glittered with the new age, the prosperity, the promise of the twenties, of the future, the parties and above all, the excesses of money, of wealth, we glittered with love.

We partied and drank love.

We would go on scavenger hunts to find books that had been thrown away. We found real treasure. With our love, we taught each other how to read and she learned to write on her own. I never quite

THE CABIN

got the hung of it, even though she desperately tried to teach me. She wanted me to
writer her love letters, but I could only whisper words of love in her ear.

When the great depression hit, we never
felt it. That's the beauty of having nothing.
When everything is taken away from you,
you suffer nothing. For once, we weren't
the poorest as one could be. Life continued
the same for us. Our love never dulled, it
only grew stronger with every second of
each day, of each night.

When we were old enough, we married
behind the church because we could not af-
ford a real wedding or anything close. Even
if we had come up with the money somehow, we were poor people, people of the
street, worthless and emotionless as rats to
society. They would have never let us
marry. We would be a disgrace to the insti-
tution. We were married in the eyes of God,

with the Bible opened between us, as his angles witness our matrimonial union. Our union was made by a small daisy flower we found, which we transformed into a ring and a passionate kiss that promised eternity.

Her memory gives me strength. My only thoughts are of her." His gaze was still far away but now filled with love and joy. He was quiet and reflective.

"What happened?" Someone asked.

His gaze turned pained like one of a tortured animal.

"World War II happened," he said.

"I had always been undesired and unwanted my whole life except when World War II happened. Suddenly I was someone. My country needed me. I needed to honor the country who abandoned me during my whole life, the country that treated me, like an animal. They offered me my one and only job I ever had.

Being a soldier.

All in uniforms, we were the same. I wasn't any different from the other. We were all just numbers. No one knew, who came from where. You could invent a complete new past and no one would know.

During the end of the war, I was deported.

She followed me.

Naturally, she would, nothing could separate us.

At night, I would sneak out of the camp base and spend nights of passion with her. I spend countless nights falling asleep with her in my arms. Feeling her body move as she breathed, was pure ecstasy.

The town had no contact with the war. The only time the town ever tasted the blood of the war was the day I lost my beautiful Antoinette.

It was a surprise attack.

It never made sense to me why they attacked the town. They had nothing to gain from it. It must have been for the pleasure of it. Maybe they got bored.

At the camp, everyone was ordered to attack back. Rumors of the horrors traveled with the winds and shortly after the wind carried the screams of the innocent townsmen. I was ordered to attack the "enemy" but my mind went to Antoinette. I needed to go look for her. I had a feeling something was wrong. But I had been ordered to fight back. In the adrenaline and confusion, I fought back until the wind whispered in my ear, the building where she was staying had been attacked.

In that second, I dropped everything and went to look for her.

I found her.

THE CABIN

She was barely alive. She was waiting for me. She knew I would look for her. She wanted to tell me she loved one last time before she departed. We had enough time to say how much we loved each other and not poverty, war, nor death could separate us.

I kissed her beautiful lips as she took in her last breath.

She was right. Of course, she was right. Of course, my Antoinette was right. Not even death could separate our love.

I love her every day like there is no tomorrow.

I do sometimes wish we could have grown old together, but when we were together, we loved each other so much, it would have lasted two complete lifetimes. We could have grown old together twice.

Now I am growing old for her, for us.

I live for her as if we were together, the way we always planned, traveling to all the places we read about when we were kids. Roaming the streets of the world, never belonging to anything but each other. Discovering everything, we could. Being happy.

I will do everything we planned until death reunites us in heaven.

I ask you, don't to look at me with pity or disgust. I never did anything to deserve this type of life. I was born into it but I am glad I was because I met Antoinette.

Together we could have got jobs, we could have gotten a house and all but to us freedom was more important. I chose this life because it makes me happy, be-cause it gives me freedom. The rest is pointless. House. Money. Cars.

THE CABIN

All I need is the memory of Antoinette," he concluded and gazed lovingly at the sky through a window.

The only name uttered during the whole night.

Antoinette.

It was also the last word spoken. He was the last person in the cabin to speak. Everyone in the cabin had spoken. In a single night they had all spoken.

Curious how the night played out.

A night they would all remember.

The silence settled around them, this time no one interrupted it. There was nothing to say. Everything that needed to be spoken had been. No one had anything to add. Their souls relaxed.

Out of everyone in the cabin, his soul was the simplest, the happiest. Always pure. It did not carry anything but love and joy. And Antoinette.

JULES PARDO

The bright moonlight dulled as he finished speaking, sensing it was longer needed.

And one by one all the burning flames burned out.

Odd.

The darkness, which followed as the last flame, died, silenced and stilled everything and everyone into a picture of thousands of words. The darkness bounded everyone in his or her seats. The silence bounded a bit of their souls together, unifying them for life.

In the little moonlight, eyes gazed into nothingness. Breathes came out slow and even. Despite it all, everyone was peaceful in his or her own way.

Some trembled with sadness, with anger.

Some smiled. Others frowned.

THE CABIN

Whatever the thought, whatever they felt, they were in it together.

In this cabin, they were equal human beings, they were all different and they all had something to say. They had more stories to tell, more thoughts, opinions and beliefs to share. They had more dreams, hopes and wishes to reveal. More doubts to manifest but they had spoken what they needed to speak to be able to find that certain peace, which now consumed their souls.

All their words floated through the cabin, making rounds throughout the cabin, playing with each other. Their words floated like ships sailing on the sea, like a feather drifting with the wind. But gradually the silence sealed them one by one into the cabin's walls.

As long as the cabin exists, the memory of them, of the night would remain.

JULES PARDO

Thoughts, thoughts, thoughts, thoughts of the future, thoughts of the past but never thoughts of the present traveled through the cabin's atmosphere.

The night was calm. The air was still. The silence an accomplice.

Chapter Eight

The sun broke slowly out of the darkness, liberating everyone from the night. The soft glow of the sun clothed their bare souls with the promised of the new day, with strength and hope. Lots of hope. The night...

It had been a night no one would forget.

Everyone had a story to tell, something to say, to be able to feel free, or maybe not to feel alone in his or her thoughts, feelings, and opinions at the end of the day. Maybe they just simply needed to be heard with no judgment, with no retaliation.

They found comfort in knowing they weren't alone. In knowing, others felt like them.

They now all shared a secret. The same different secret. Their own secret mixed with the others, creating individual secrets with different meanings but with the same words. The same secret which traveled around the cabin was unique and only theirs.

No one would ever tell. It was too private. Too personal.

Many thoughts would have been trapped forever in their souls if it had not been for the storm tearing them apart, pushing them to the cabin and finally into the dead calmness of the night.

Many thoughts keep private for fear of the reaction they may cause.

THE CABIN

Many thoughts screaming to be heard, to be acknowledged. And finally being heard, being acknowledged.

It lifted weights of their souls, only leaving the promise of cherished silence of the night.

As everyone regained their strength, they rested in their seats, content and full of life. Whatever happened from now on, they would be prepared. They had all survived the storm, which almost destroyed them physically, but most importantly, they had survived the night. The night where despair went hand in hand with doom.

They had survived their own inner demons and angels.

With the new day, they had been liberated from their demons as their angels took over promising a better life.

They began looking at each other, smiling like accomplices.

They had done it.

They began conversing between them, some getting up and forming small groups. They exchanged names, smiles, a few laughs here and there and hope. Hope everything would be okay. People walked from group to group meeting everyone. As the sun settled in the sky, they all formed small groups, in which they were most comfortable in.

They asked and answered questions.

They told new stories.

The cabin hummed with their voices, the wind carrying it past the meadows to someplace far away. Maybe someone would hear the wind whisper their excitement, their sympathy, their existence, their survival and their unbreakable union.

On one side of the cabin, the young woman with passionate eyes stood closely discussing with the young handsome man. They never looked anywhere but into each other's eyes. The promise of devotion and love sparkled in their eyes. They were in their own world. Creating their future, creating their past as each second went by. Nothing would break their connection.

The homeless man stood in front of a window, contempt and gaze far away. The young woman who, when feeling threatened by other women's beauty or intelligence wanted to destroy them, went to stand by him gazing far away too. He turned to study her as she looked up. Tears formed in her eyes and through a shaky voice, she said, "I just want a man to love me the same way you love your wife. I... I want to be the most beautiful and intelligent woman in his eyes" a tear rolled down her cheek. He nodded and looked outside once more, so did she. Silence stretch out between them until he told her another story of Antoinette. Afterwards, she told another story about herself. They swapped stories never looking at each other but giving each other strength.

The young woman who was mistreated by her boyfriend sat talking animatedly with the man who hoped to find a woman who would see past his outbursts. He sat protectively over her, while her tender smile caressed him and accepted him. Small sparks flew between them until, with any warning, a fire of passion, tenderness and true love ignited between them. An invisible and unbreakable bond linking them together. Their past slowly being forgotten in the vast sea of forgotten memories.

The CEO sat giving out tips, telling stories to a couple of small groups who came by to listen closely, to be inspired.

THE CABIN

The woman who was pregnant sat on her husband lap, talking names and plans for their baby. Her husband was always touching and rubbing her stomach. He was so happy that it was hard from him to keep his smile off his face. Every now and then, he would abruptly kiss her belly with so much tenderness then kiss her passionately and whisper lovingly, looking straight into her eyes. They were also in their own world.

On the other side of the cabin, three men stood talking, exchanging their experiences, advices and questions.

Not far from them, the man who had been to jail, the man who was always angry and the young woman who hated her body stood towards the middles of the cabin, laughing and telling more stories. The feeling of frustration, of feelings judged bonded them together.

A few hours went by and nothing changed except some groups became bigger while other smaller and new ones formed.

It all stayed relatively the same but now some began to look outside the window. They wondered if they would be able to leave the cabin. Would someone rescue them or would they be here until the snow melted? Would they be able to survive until the snow melted enough for them to leave?

The long night began to wear them down. They were hungry and tired. Not the best combination. The hum of the conversation dulled. Here and there, people stilled whispered to one another but the rest went back to their seats and sat contemplating what would happen.

They looked out the windows and still hoped.

THE CABIN

An hour went by and nothing. By now, the conversation had stopped completely.

Everyone was worried. Thoughts turned negative despite it all, despite all the hope which the new day promised. The silence settled once more on the cabin but outside birds chirped and sang making everything more bearable. It gave them the hope, which was slowly disappearing.

The sun warmed the cabin through the windows, giving everyone a little bit of color to their pale complexions.

From afar, they heard their salvation. A divine salvation. The birds around the cabin began chanting their melodies louder and sweeter. Everyone heard far away engines soaring through the snow becoming louder and louder.

They got up and ran to the windows on the right, where the sound was coming from. Some squealed in excitement seeing their salvation. Other tried desperately to peer over the shoulder of those in front of them. Some relaxed and looked up and mouthed "thank you" with their hand pressed to their hearts in gratitude. Some embraced each other.

Everyone was happy, smiling and radiating.

Hope was restored.

The engine stopped and everyone held his or her breath. Total silence in gulped them. Outside the birds stopped chanting.

In the silence, a strong male voice yelled, "HELLO, ANYONE HERE?"

It took everyone a second to find their voices and then they began shouting back.

"YES!" "HELP US!" "WE ARE IN HERE!" "HELP!"

THE CABIN

In the next minutes, which followed, they heard snow being shoveled away from the entrance, commands being shouted and sweet commotion of life.

Then the doors opened.

The light infiltrated the cabin quickly with the wind. Together, they caressed every inch of the cabin, every person.

Everyone exhaled relieved.

Police officers and firefighters stood by the doors waiting for them as some began gathering and putting on their coats while those who kept them on headed towards the doors. Everything was in order until someone yelled, "STOP!"

Everyone froze. Some in mid-action. The police officers and firefighters stood by the doors confused but ready for whatever might happen next. The police officers' hand twitched towards their guns.

JULES PARDO

The person who yelled turned to stare at the back corner of the cabin and asked gently "You never talked, what's your story?"

Everyone turned to stare at me.

They murmured in agreement. Some mumbled the same question here and there. Some were surprised to see me. They stared at me asking again the same question, curiosity burning in their eyes. I looked at every one of them.

"My story is your story."

Epilogue

I watched them leave together. I watched them embark on a new journey. I watched the new couples hold hands, determined to move forwards together, to never let go and to vanquish the past with love. I watched them walk among each other tired and animatedly quite.

I watched them leave.

I watched them pass through the door, leaving behind their doubts, their fears, their frustration and everything that haunted them.

It was all left behind.

I watched them leave with satisfaction tattooed to their faces. Joy, love and hope settle any vacant spot their souls had.

They walked out without looking back.

The cabin was now empty. I looked around the place, at all the candles, which had lit our night. Now they were all melted away, only remaining what had been. I gazed at the seats where they had all once been, where their memory would remain. Sunrays shone on their seats.

Humph...

My story... My story... My story...

My story is the same as yours, as his, as hers. I am like them. I am like you. I have a story which yours, he, her and ours. I have my own story, although I prefer yours than mine.

My story is I am.

I am the stranger you pass by one the street. I am a son. I am a friend, a lover. I am one more person on the earth. I am one more human being. I exist. I roam the streets, the cities, the towns and villages. I belong nowhere and everywhere. There is a little bit of my soul in every place I have been and will be. I am here and there. I am me. I am the one you ignore, the one you notice. I am a listener. I am an observer.

I am a man. I am like everyone.

But I don't feel.

I observe detached from emotions. I only observe emotions govern others. I see pain, joy and love. I see all types of relationships in all their glories and defeats. I see you, him and her. I see individuals. I see nations. I observe. It's all I can do. It's all I need to do. I observe them and us. I stand in front of my reflection for hours and observe myself. I observe everything like watching a movie or like reading a book. I observe humanity without judgment or prejudice. I see it the way it is. I observe everything the way it is.

I think. I try to analyze the situation, the moment. I question. I try to understand. I compile all the knowledge of life as I can. I live in my mind, in my thoughts...

I guess that is my story. Being and observing is my story. I feel no pain nor joy. I neither hate nor love. I am neither the past nor the present nor the future. I observe the now, the past, the future.

I am.

A firefighter came back.

"Sir, are you coming?" He asked. His voice was familiar; he must have been the one who had yelled earlier.

"Yes, of course." I replied.

As I stepped outside, the sweet wind whispered in my ear. I looked back at the cabin. I can see the whole night replay itself in my mind.

THE CABIN

In the truck, I remembered the nights every detail until the bumpy ride came to a halt bring me back to the present.

A memory indeed I will recall for the rest of my existence.

As I step out of the truck, the wind whispers in my ear once again. I close my eyes as the sweet wind tenderly caresses my face, making my head turn left. I open my eyes and turn my body to face that direction. I then walk without hesitation towards that direction.

The sun is shining, the sky is blue with puffy white clouds, the air cool and sweet and the day lively agitated.

I wander into my next story.

Acknowledgments

I would like to thank my mother first of all, for always being there for me. Thank you so much for believing in me, even when I didn't. Thank you for understanding me. I couldn't have done this without your support. I am forever grateful. I love you.

Second of all, I would like to thank my brother for seeing the writer in me, long before I did. Thank you for you giving the best advice when I most desperately needed it and for your support. I love you.

Lastly, I would like to thank whoever you are. Thank you for taking time out of your life, to read my novella. I appreciate with all my heart. I hope you enjoyed it as much as I did writing it. Thank You.

Thank You

♥

About The Author

Always with a notebook in hand and traveling through the universe of her thoughts,
Jules Pardo is from everywhere and nowhere.

Photo: © Esperanza Sanchez Espitia